LIVE
FROM BRENTWOOD HIGH

Sarah's Dilemma

Live! From Brentwood High

FROM BRENTWOOD HIGH

Sarah's Dilemma

JUDY BAER

BETHANY HOUSE PUBLISHERS
MINNEAPOLIS, MINNESOTA 55438

Sarah's Dilemma
Judy Baer

Cover illustration by Joe Nordstrom

Library of Congress Catalog Card Number 95–24615

ISBN 1–55661–389–X

Published by Bethany House Publishers
A Ministry of Bethany Fellowship, Inc.
11300 Hampshire Avenue South
Minneapolis, Minnesota 55438

Printed in the United States of America

For the dedicated staff
at the North Dakota State Library.

Special thanks to those reference librarians
who help me with my research.

JUDY BAER received a B.A. in English and Education from Concordia College in Moorhead, Minnesota. She has had over thirty novels published and is a member of the National Romance Writers of America, the Society of Children's Book Writers, and the National Federation of Press Women.

Two of her novels, *Adrienne* and *Paige*, have been prizewinning bestsellers in the Bethany House SPRINGFLOWER SERIES (for girls 12–15). Both books have been awarded first place for juvenile fiction in the National Federation of Press Women's communications contest.

LIVE
FROM BRENTWOOD HIGH

CHAPTER 1

LIVE

FROM BRENTWOOD HIGH

"Look out! Coming through!" The honking sound of a cheap toy horn challenged the noise of Chaos Central. "Out of my way!" Everyone in the media room turned to see who—or what—was coming through the door.

Sarah Riley rolled into the room with a theatrical flair, squeezing an orange rubber globe attached to the little black horn that was making such a racket. Her red hair looked windblown, as though she'd put her wheelchair into warp speed down the halls of Brentwood High. The vehicle in question was decorated with foil-covered blazes of mock lightning.

"Am I late?"

"For the moon shot? Yes. The rocket left fifteen minutes ago. Of course, I suppose you could blast off in that thing." Izzy Mooney sauntered over to Sarah, a half-eaten candy bar in his hand. "What's with the horn?"

"I was late for class twice yesterday. Too much congestion in the halls. I decided that if I didn't want any more tardy slips, I would have to take matters into my own hands." Sarah honked the tinny-sounding horn. "What do you think?"

"I know *I'd* get out of your way," Jake Saunders said, dimples flashing deep in his cheeks.

"Good. Then it works." Sarah relaxed against the back of her chair. She was dressed in a bright orange jacket and equally vibrant yellow turtleneck above her blue jeans. Her socks matched her outfit—one was yellow, the other orange. The vivid colors highlighted the warm red of her hair and the pale ivory of her skin. Sarah looked as cheerful as she sounded.

"Hi, Julie. What's happening? Molly, I love your outfit! Josh, new haircut?" She wheeled her way around the room greeting the student staff of *Live! From Brentwood High.*

Her characteristic good humor was met with something less than warmth.

"Who put a quarter in you, Riley? Hasn't anyone told you it's morning?" Kate Akima's dark eyes glittered unpleasantly. "I don't like when people are too cheerful before noon."

"I think she put too much sugar on her cereal. She's on a high," Andrew Tremaine concluded. "She'll get over it."

"What's with you people today?" Sarah asked, unoffended by the response of her friends and co-workers. This crew worked together for the student-run television station at Brentwood High. They'd all seen each other in far worse moods than this.

"I wish you wouldn't be so cheerful all the time," Molly muttered. "You put the rest of us to shame. I was just complaining about what an awful day it is and then you roll in acting like it's the best day of the year!"

Julie Osborn, whom Izzy had once deemed the "Official Pain in the Neck" of the media room, scowled at Sarah. "Some days you're so sweet you give me cavities, Riley. Today's one of those days." Julie paused to consider. "It's that Christian stuff with you, isn't it?"

Sarah burst out laughing. The only admitted Christian on the television staff, she was an oddity to most of the students. Every time Sarah did something unexpected, her friends blamed it on the fact that either (a) she was a Christian, or (b) she used a wheelchair.

"Actually, it's more the fact that I'm a morning person, Julie. My mom's a Christian, but even she can't smile until she's had her morning coffee."

"Then I like your mother. Anyone who's grumpy in the morning can't be all bad."

"Ignore them," Darby Ellison advised as she walked toward Sarah. "There must be a change in the weather. Everybody is crabby today."

"She'll be crabby too once she hears what Ms. Wright has planned for us," Kate warned dourly. "Just wait."

"So what's the bad news? Are we covering toxic waste?"

"Worse. She says we have to start doing reviews—both for the television show and for the newspaper." In addition to the weekly *Live! From Brentwood High* student-run cable television show, the class also produced a small paper and an occasional in-school radio show. None of the students were as enthused about these projects as they were about the TV show, and they let it be known when assignments were made.

"What kind of reviews? Books? Movies?"

"Now the news gets *really* horrible. We have to review a *play*."

"What's so bad about that? I love plays."

"You would," Julie grumbled. "There's a new production opening at that old theater downtown. You know the one, it looks like Shakespeare used it for his own plays—when he was still alive."

"I can't believe Ms. Wright would make us go to that mousetrap and sit through some boring garbage! There are three new movies opening at the Cineplex and we're stuck going to the theater." Andrew looked disgusted, as if someone had made a royal infringement on his time.

"Well, I think it sounds like fun!" Sarah said. "What about you, Darby?"

"It's fine with me. I don't have an allergy to culture like these illiterates do."

"Call me whatever you want," Julie said haughtily. "Just don't make me go."

"We have ten tickets," Darby explained. "Ms. Wright wants us to use them all. We're supposed to work in teams of two on the reviews. A 'thumbs up, thumbs down' sort of thing. Four will do the package for the TV show, the rest will do a column for the paper."

"Who's going?"

"So far, no one. We need volunteers."

"Count me out," Kate chimed. "I wouldn't go into that old rat-infested theater for anything."

"It's being renovated."

"That probably means they boarded the rats into the walls."

"Gross! I'm not going either," Julie announced.

"*I* think it sounds like fun!" Sarah said. "I'll go. We can't let free tickets go to waste. But I don't want to go alone. I haven't driven much in that part of town. Who'll go with me?"

"Count me in," Darby said.

"If Darby is going, I'll go," Jake Saunders piped. He was one of the best-looking guys in Brentwood, and no one—especially Darby—had missed that fact.

"I suppose I should go too," Molly Ashton said. "One way to get into Hollywood is to be discovered on stage. Maybe I'll decide to start out as a stage actress." Molly's future plan was to be a model or movie star. It was, in fact, the main reason she'd signed up for the television production class. She was eager to learn whatever she could about what she referred to as "the business."

"You're going?" Andrew Tremaine looked dismayed. He'd been trying to get on Molly's good side for a long time. It was apparent in his expression that if he *did* volunteer to attend the theater, it would be for only one reason—to be closer to Molly.

At that moment, *Live's!* advisor, Rosie Wright, breezed into the room in a cloud of perfume and chalk dust. She was wearing a gauzy one-piece dress that looked very much like a small, belted tent. Huge brass earrings hung to her shoulders, and her brown hair swung in a braid. "Well, have you decided yet?" she asked abruptly.

"Decided what?"

"Who's going to the theater. I just talked to Gary Richmond and he said he'd like to go if there are still tickets available." Gary, Ms. Wright's assistant and resident cameraman, was as unique and unorthodox as Rosie.

"So far it's Sarah, Darby, Molly, Jake, and Andrew."

"And us," Kate and Julie chimed.

Everyone in the room stared at them. Julie shrugged helplessly, "What's a little old rat compared to a party? If everyone else is going, we want to go too."

"Izzy, Josh, does that include you?" Ms. Wright skewered the pair with a look.

Josh's black curly head bobbed.

Izzy groaned. "I'm not very cultural, Ms. Wright. Last time I tried something 'edifying,' they had to close the museum."

"What does 'edifying' mean? That you ate the museum?" Andrew looked annoyed, as he often did when Izzy used words unfamiliar to his vocabulary.

Though Izzy often *looked* as rumpled as a pile of unfolded clothes on an unmade bed and about as intelligent as cauliflower, under that thick skull and buzz-cut hair he housed the IQ of a genius.

"Edifying: uplifting, educational, enlightening, instructional," Izzy recited.

"Thank you, Mr. Webster," Andrew sneered. "I knew that all along. I just didn't think *you* knew it."

"Yeah, right."

"You'd better tell us *why* they closed the museum, Isador." Ms. Wright looked both amused and dismayed. Izzy had an unfortunate way of unintentionally causing disruptions which could lead to the closing of large, important buildings.

"Just a little something with the lighting system and the elevator. I was curious to see how it was all wired. How was I supposed to know it was that easy to trip the switches? Some electrical engineer made a really poor mistake. . . ."

"Perhaps Gary *should* go with you." Ms. Wright looked understandably worried. She turned to the silent and aloof member of the team sitting near the window. "Shane? How about you?"

"No way. I'm not the theater type. Besides, I'm going to do some editing. Let someone else go." A familiar sullen expression settled on Shane's features that signaled to everyone in the room that he would not attend the play.

The fact that Shane was even *in* the production class was something of a minor miracle according to those who knew him. Restless, brooding, and occasionally on the fringe of trouble, Shane was hard to get to know and even harder to befriend. He'd developed aloofness to an art form. Still, more than once, it had been Shane who'd given the group direction for their investigative news reports. "Street smart" was the best way to describe him.

He raked his fingers through his straight, dark blond hair. "Just watch out where you park downtown. Use one of the public lots and get under a street light if you can. There are some bad kids hanging out down there."

No one questioned him. Shane had grown up without a father in his life and too little parental monitoring. There'd probably been a time not too long ago when *he'd* been one of the bad kids hanging out in the uptown area.

"Oh no!" Izzy catapulted out of his chair in front of the graphics generator. "I forgot to watch the time! I have to get to Home Living class. We're finishing our unit on Italian cooking today and we're doing a special red sauce for the spaghetti." An expression of bliss settled across his features. "Fresh tomatoes, garlic, onion . . . it's going to be great. Great? Grate! I'm in charge of the fresh Parmesan. I have to get it grated before class."

"The only reason you even enrolled in Home Living was so you could eat the food," Andrew sneered. "The school food budget has probably gone up ten percent since you started that class."

Izzy didn't make any denials or explanations. Instead he allowed a brief smile to grace his quirky features. "It's my favorite class. Where else could you get easy A's and great food at the same time?"

"As if that's a big concern to you," Darby chastised. "You're an honors student. You could be taking all advanced classes!"

"I'm taking enough of them," Izzy said. "The food . . . I mean, Home Living is a good break in the day."

"He's bright enough to take advanced chemistry and physics," Kate pointed out. "But what does he make a big deal about getting? A spot in the kitchen.

Great foresight, Izzy. You'll make some woman a wonderful wife."

"You won't cook all year, will you?" Darby asked. "There must be *other* units. Do you have to sew?"

Izzy looked startled, as though he hadn't considered the possibility that he might have to learn to do something other than cook. "Maybe. It doesn't matter. The teacher's pretty cool. I like the class. Besides, there's nothing about a Home Living class that could be too hard for me, right? What could be so bad?" He glanced at the clock. "Gotta go. Otherwise I might miss the salad. See you later."

"Someday Izzy is going to outsmart himself," Sarah predicted with a mischievous smirk.

CHAPTER 2

LIVE

FROM BRENTWOOD HIGH

The media room was quiet when Darby peeked her head inside the door after school. Only Sarah was there, poring over information about the new "toaster" which had just been installed. The toaster was actually a high-tech computer for doing amazing things—like swap the heads of the talent while they were reading the news or morph humans into animals. Izzy was the one most familiar with the toaster, but Sarah had expressed an interest as well.

Sarah looked up from her book. Her expression was solemn and her eyes, usually so bright and inquisitive, seemed cloudy. "Just a little cramming. Izzy and Gary are going to show me how to run this thing soon, and I don't want to sound like an idiot. I think I must be the only non-computer nerd in the world to tackle something like this."

"You'll do fine. You always do."

"Right."

Darby frowned. Sarah was considerably more subdued than she'd been this morning. She appeared tired and a little sad. The horn she'd been using to get through the halls all day was jammed into the book bag attached to her wheelchair. She reminded Darby of a wilted flower.

"What's wrong?"

"I can't remember all these technical terms," Sarah said. "It's like learning a new language."

"Not about the toaster," Darby chided. "What's wrong with *you?*"

"Me? Nothing." A wisp of a smile flickered on Sarah's features, then vanished.

"I don't believe that for a minute," Darby persisted, alarmed. This behavior wasn't like Sarah at all.

"It's nothing I want to talk about, okay? I'm just in a weird mood." Sarah pushed herself away from the table. "Maybe it's time to go home. Need a ride?"

"I suppose. Just take me to your house and I'll walk from there." Darby followed Sarah out the door to the parking lot where her customized van waited. Deftly Sarah maneuvered her wheelchair onto the lift and into the driver's seat. Darby clamored in after her.

The inside of the van was typically Sarah. There was a fuzzy panda bear stuck to the windshield with suction cups on its feet and the Bible verse, "For God so loved the world that He gave His only Son, that whoever believes in Him shall not perish but have eternal life." It was printed in calligraphy and taped to the dash.

"Buckle up," Sarah ordered. "First rule of the 'Dream Machine.'" Obediently Darby complied.

They talked little on the way to the Riley's home, a sprawling ranch house on a street not many blocks from Darby's own home.

"Are you sure you don't want me to take you all the way home?" Sarah asked. "No problem."

"The exercise will do me good. I was just too lazy to walk all the way from school. I appreciate the lift."

"Want to come inside for a few minutes?" Sarah's voice sounded both tentative and hopeful.

Darby looked at her and saw the unsureness in Sarah's eyes. "Sure, I'd love to."

The Riley house was completely wheelchair accessible. Sarah grasped the push rims on her chair to roll up the sloping ramp to the front door. She leaned forward to open it. Darby followed her inside, looking around but trying not to be too obvious.

The house was spacious and nicely decorated. There were hardwood floors everywhere and no rugs—an obvious concession to Sarah's chair. The doorways were wide and furniture was set so that it would be easy to maneuver a wheel chair through any of the rooms.

"Want some lemonade or something?" Sarah wondered.

"Whatever you've got."

Together the girls found not only beverages but also a container of crackers and a can of what Sarah referred to as "squirtable cheese." When they were settled at the kitchen table, Darby put her elbows on the table, propped her chin in her hands and said, "All right, *now* will you tell me what's wrong?"

Sarah nibbled on a cracker and considered the question. "You won't think I'm stupid?"

"Not likely. I suppose I can't be sure until I hear what's wrong, but I'd practically bet my life on the fact that you aren't stupid."

Sarah smiled. "Thanks for the vote of confidence, I think." She ground the remains of her cracker between her fingers and watched the crumbs fall to the tabletop.

"I feel very selfish and self-centered saying this, but I've been feeling . . . lonely."

Darby tipped her head to one side but didn't speak.

"Maybe lonely isn't quite the right word. Maybe 'left out' is better." Sarah looked downcast. "I even hate saying it because it sounds so selfish, but it's been bothering me a lot lately. Jake likes you. Andrew has a crush on Molly. Everyone in school seems to have dates on the weekends. But no one even *looks* at me!" Sarah flushed until her cheeks were nearly as red as her hair. "I'm almost seventeen years old and I've never even *had* a date!"

Darby was dumbstruck. Sarah had taken her completely by surprise. "Really?" she finally blurted. "But you're so pretty!"

Then Darby clamped a hand over her mouth. "Sorry I sounded so surprised, but you're one of the nicest, most attractive girls I've ever met. I guess I just thought. . . ."

"That I'd have a life outside of school?" Sarah looked rueful. "I wish."

"It doesn't make sense," Darby said. "What's *wrong* with the guys at Brentwood High? They're missing something special if they haven't noticed you!"

"It's the chair. I'm sure that's it. Why would a guy

want to take me out when it involves all these pounds
of metal, my customized van, a big hassle and usually
a bunch of unwanted attention while I'm trying to get
in and out of a movie theater or a restaurant? They
all probably realize how embarrassing it would be. I
hate it but I've got no choice!"

"Do you really think that's it? I can't believe every
guy is so shallow that he can't get past the chair."
Darby frowned furiously. "Creeps."

"Don't be so hard on them, Darby. I probably
shouldn't even be hurt by it. Most guys our age are
interested in girls who look good, girls who are popular. I don't fit into either category. Guys don't even
think of me as someone to date."

"That's not true! You're *beautiful*, Sarah. Inside
and out!" Tears stung Darby's eyes as she looked at
the other girl's sad expression. "It's not your fault
that teenaged boys are immature jerks!"

Sarah chuckled in spite of herself. "Thanks for
coming to my defense. I was having a pity party today
and needed to whine a little, that's all. I'm over it now.
All I needed was someone to listen."

"Not so fast," Darby said. "You can't get over
something that easily. Quit trying to be brave, Sarah.
You have every right to be bummed by this. I apologize for being so thoughtless. You're so cheerful and
upbeat around the studio that I never think of you as
having any problems. I've been a lousy friend. I'd like
to make it up to you. You're so nice . . ."

"Fun. Nice. Pleasant. Cheerful. That's me. I'm also
trapped in this chair. Guys don't think of me as a real
girl, Darby. I'm a personality in a cage and the chair

is the cage." Sarah curled her fist in frustration. "What no one seems to realize is that other than this chair, I'm a perfectly normal teenager! I like guys, music, and fashion. I enjoy changing my hair and sitting at the beach. I paint my fingernails and read half the night. I'm *normal* and no one knows it!"

Sarah's shoulders drooped as she sat in her chair. She *did* look trapped. Darby reached out and touched her wrist.

"I never knew. I never understood. But if I can change my attitude, others can too."

"I don't want you to say anything."

"Then how. . . ."

"Nothing, Darby. Not a word. You've *got* to promise me that you won't say anything to anyone about what I've told you. I might be feeling left out and sorry for myself but I also feel very embarrassed and selfish. Lots of people have problems worse than mine. It seems very self-centered of me to wish I were more popular." Sarah flushed. "It's just that sometimes I feel so lonely. . . ."

Darby was overcome with dismay. Sarah Riley was one of the sweetest, nicest, kindest people at Brentwood High. She was always friendly, encouraging and cheerful. She was so *uncomplaining* about her disability and her life that it probably had never occurred to anyone that she might be unhappy.

"I can't believe I've been so stupid!" Darby exclaimed.

"You aren't stupid."

"Yes, I am. You always seem so together that I never thought about you and guys . . . and the wheelchair. Every *other* girl in school thinks about boys. Why *not* you?"

Darby's expression of dismay deepened. "But that's just what you're talking about, isn't it? People treat you differently and even think of you differently because you're in a wheelchair. You'd be weird if you *didn't* want to date. I'm sorry, Sarah, I've always thought I treated you just like I treat everyone else, but I guess it's not true. I assumed that because you were in a wheelchair you just weren't interested in. . . ." Her voice trailed away.

Sarah expelled a puffy little breath of exasperation. "What am I going to do, Darby? I'm stuck in this chair and there's no way out. Am I ever going to have a boyfriend? Will some guy notice me and not the metal I'm sitting in? Or will I have to spend my whole life alone?"

Darby shrugged helplessly, at a loss for an answer.

"Now I'm sounding really dramatic," Sarah said with a weak laugh. "You caught me at a bad moment. I'm not usually this self-absorbed. I apologize."

Darby waved away Sarah's statement. "The guys in the *Live! From Brentwood High* program aren't scared of you. They don't avoid you or treat you any differently than they treat the rest of us."

"They don't ask me out on dates either."

"True. It's as if they treat you as one of the guys." Darby snapped her fingers. "That's *it!* They treat you like another guy. You're a buddy!"

"So? I like that. It makes me feel normal."

"Don't you see? They think of you as a friend, but not as a *girl*." Darby chewed her lower lip as she contemplated the situation. "I think we can fix this problem."

Sarah looked startled. "You do?"

"Sure. We just have to subtly remind the guys that you're a girl."

"They should be able to see that for themselves."

"An *available* girl. A dateable girl."

"And how are we supposed to do that?" Sarah looked amused. "Put a sign on my forehead that says 'Saturday night is open'?"

"Something like that."

"You're kidding!"

Darby grinned. "Only a little bit. Really, the first thing we should do is change your look."

"What's wrong with my look?"

"Nothing. But change always attracts attention. Have you got a curling iron and a ponytail holder?" Darby eyed Sarah's beautiful red hair. "We'll start at the top and work down."

While Darby was making soft red curls all over Sarah's head, Sarah paged through a catalogue pointing at outfits. "That one?"

"Too plain."

"This?"

"Too frilly."

"How about. . . ."

"Wrong color. You need to wear something teal colored or emerald green. With your coloring that will be spectacular."

"I do have a new sweater in my closet. It looks something like this." Sarah pointed to an attractive outfit on the page. "I'd planned to wear it with a long black skirt and boots."

"Perfect. I'll do your hair. You'll be spectacular. If the guys don't notice a change in you, I'll take them all in for eye exams."

"Don't be too optimistic," Sarah warned. "This wheelchair is a pretty big barrier. It's hard to see around, if you understand what I mean."

"But it can be done. The guys at Brentwood High have been taking you for granted and it's time that stopped."

Darby fluffed a curl into place and stepped back to look at her handiwork. "Awesome! You have the best bone-structure. Why didn't I realize that before?"

Sarah's appreciative smile left Darby glowing as well. It was definitely time that the guys of Brentwood High began to realize that Sarah was a girl with feelings too. With a conspiratorial air, Darby pushed Sarah toward her room to get the sweater. Those boys were never going to know what hit them!

CHAPTER **3**

LIVE

FROM BRENTWOOD HIGH

"Izzy, you clean up pretty well!" Jake observed as they met in the media room.

Everyone was dressed up for the play, but Izzy had gone all out for the occasion with a navy blue suit, white shirt and colorful polka-dotted bow tie. He'd even moussed his buzz-cut hair into obedient little spikes.

"My grandmother made me do it," he admitted. "And my twin sisters did my hair. The only thing I got to pick out for myself was my tie." He fingered the garish fabric affectionately.

"It figures," Josh muttered under his breath to Darby.

"You look pretty sharp yourself," Darby said to the African-American boy. "Great sweater."

"Thanks. It's a birthday gift."

"Did you have a birthday recently? We didn't celebrate it in Chaos Central."

Josh looked shyly at his shoes. "It's tomorrow."

Darby clapped her hands. "Listen up, everyone. It's Josh's birthday tomorrow!" Immediately the group broke into a rousing, off-key rendition of "Happy Birthday."

"I hate to break up this musical happening," Gary announced into the din, "but Sarah's waiting outside in her van. She's got room for six and I'll take three of you with me."

"Kate and I will go with Gary," Julie chimed. "The rest of you can go with Sarah."

No one argued. Everyone knew that Julie didn't want to lower herself to being squeezed into the van for the drive. It might wrinkle her dress. Worse yet, she might not be able to make the proper entrance at the theater if she were crammed into the back of a van with a group of teenagers. Appearances were very important to Julie.

Darby winked at Sarah as she climbed into the van. Sarah's hair looked spectacular. Her curls were glinting red in the fading evening light. They framed her face giving her a wide-eyed look. The teal sweater accentuated her pale beauty. Sarah was stunning.

"Let me get in first. I'll crawl to the back. Darby, do you want to sit on my lap. . . ." Izzy stopped mid-tease to stare at Sarah. "What happened to you?"

Sarah feigned innocence but her eyes sparkled. "Why? Am I late?"

"No, not that. What happened to *you?* Your hair. . . ."

"Darby fixed it for me. Do you like it?"

"Yeah. Lots. It makes you look . . . different."

"Different? Is that all you can say?" Molly elbowed Izzy in the side. "She looks spectacular! Really hot. I love it!"

Even Andrew Tremaine, who followed Molly into the van, nodded. "Looks good. And I like the sweater. Get out of the way, Mooney. What do you think you are—furniture?"

Izzy stumbled to the back seat with his head still turned toward Sarah as though he couldn't quite believe what he was seeing. When Darby got in the van, she gave Sarah a thumbs up sign and winked. The plan was working. Just the look on Sarah's face was enough to make Darby smile.

"Nice outfit," Jake commented to Sarah as he jumped into the van. "Looks good. Everybody in? Where's Josh?"

Josh appeared just as Jake spoke. "I almost forgot my notebook . . . Hey, Sarah, I like it!"

As she pulled away from the curb, Sarah was grinning broadly.

————

The Madison theater was one of the oldest buildings in Brentwood. It was being restored bit by bit as money became available. The face of the building was the last thing to be renovated so it still appeared somewhat shabby. However, there were limousines pulling up to the curb and people in formal dress going into the theater.

"I'm glad Grandma made me wear my suit," Izzy breathed. "This looks pretty fancy-smancy to me."

Sarah parked the van near a street light as Shane had suggested and, when her passengers had alighted, maneuvered herself onto the lift and down to street level.

"That's pretty neat," Izzy commented, studying the mechanism. "Maybe when I have some free time, you'd let me take a look at that and see how it works."

"Don't let him, Sarah. Before you know it, he'll be trying to take it apart and you'll be left without a vehicle. We know you too well, Mooney."

Longingly Izzy eyed the lift, but he didn't argue. His reputation preceded him. With a sigh, he put his hands on the handles of Sarah's wheelchair and steered her toward the theater.

Gary, Julie, and Kate were already there. Gary had the tickets in his hands. One of the quaint features of the old theater was an outdoor ticket office covered with an ornate gilded canopy. As the group approached, the woman in the ticket window stared at Sarah with dismay.

"Is something wrong?" Gary asked as the woman gave a small, distressed gasp. "Seating problems?"

"You didn't tell me you had someone in a wheelchair in your party." The woman sounded accusing.

"Excuse me?" Gary frowned. "What does that have to do with anything?"

"We aren't wheelchair accessible yet. That portion of our renovation is scheduled to begin later this month. We just received funding to make the building handicapped accessible." She nodded toward the theater entrance. There were several steps to climb. "We've been using an old service elevator in the back for wheelchairs, but it's broken."

Sarah looked crushed. She slumped in her chair. "It's okay. I'll go home and be back to pick you up when the play is over," she murmured. "Tell me what time I should be here."

"No way." Izzy sounded angry.

"You can't *all* skip the production. Take notes for me. Tell me what to say in my review. I should be able to write it anyway."

Izzy ignored her and turned to the woman at the ticket window. "Are there more steps inside?"

"A few."

"Could we carry her in?"

The woman looked startled. "I suppose you could, but I'm not sure. . . ."

"Then that's what we'll do. That is, Sarah, if you don't mind."

Now it was Sarah's turn to look startled. "Carry me?"

"There are five of us. We're strong. We can lift you up and down the steps, no problem. If you'll agree, that is."

Sarah looked longingly at the marquee. It was obvious that she wanted very much to attend the play. Suddenly, she smiled. "Oh, why not? Just don't drop me."

Darby and Molly held their breath as Jake, Izzy, Gary, and Josh bent to pick up Sarah's chair. Andrew stood behind, ready to brace the back if it tipped. Much as she was trying to look confident, it was apparent that Sarah felt both self-conscious and apprehensive at the turn the evening had taken.

Worse yet, their predicament was drawing a crowd. Several theater-goers were shaking their heads and softly discussing the situation. It seemed as though the whole world was focused on the little group of teenagers. Izzy and the others were oblivious, however, to everything but Sarah. With the gallantry of five Sir Galahads they swept her up the stairs and through the double doors to the theater.

Darby and the other girls scrambled to follow. When they caught up, the men were settling Sarah on the floor. The relief on her face mingled with a smile as Izzy stood in front of her and took a courtly bow.

"Are you all right?" Molly wondered as the others went to check out the rest of the theater.

Sarah nodded. "It's pretty scary being lifted in the air like that, being totally out of control. I really do have a fear of falling or being dropped, but it worked out fine. The guys were very sweet."

A tear glistened on the tip of her eyelash. "I was so afraid I'd have to go home and miss the play. I think I would have let them carry me half a mile just to be here!"

Molly and Darby exchanged a sympathetic glance, trying to imagine a little of what Sarah must be feeling. Kate and Julie had wandered off to the ladies room.

Gary and the others returned shortly with grim expressions on their faces.

"Now what?" Molly blurted.

"There's no space for Sarah's chair except at the end of our row. It should work out, though, if you don't mind." Gary turned to Sarah.

She shrugged. "I've come this far. I'm not going back now. It'll be fine."

It wasn't exactly "fine," but with some maneuvering of the chair, they got Sarah settled. Fortunately the aisle was wide and her chair didn't block traffic. Izzy crouched on the seat next to her like a big guard dog and scowled at everyone who passed and looked as though they might say something about the wheelchair being in the way.

"They'd better get going on this handicapped accessible stuff soon," Gary said with a grimace. "This is ridiculous."

"I never realized before tonight what kinds of things Sarah must have to go through," Jake commented. "I assumed the chair was a pain in the neck, but this . . ."

"I'm amazed that Sarah is as cheerful as she is. I haven't heard her complain once! When you lifted her chair her fingers tightened on the arm until they started to turn white but she didn't say anything. I never realized how much she's at the mercy of other people," Darby said.

Jake frowned. "What if we'd dropped her?"

"You wouldn't have."

"I suppose not. We're all strong and athletic, but still . . ."

Darby put her hand over Jake's as it lay on the arm rest between them. She understood just how he felt. She, too, was coming to realize what kind of life Sarah lived.

A scuffle at the end of their row interrupted their thoughts.

"Hey! Get out of the way!" The words were thick and slurred and the man who spoke them appeared to have been drinking. He weaved down the aisle and managed to stub his toe on the locked wheel of Sarah's chair. "What are you doing sitting in the middle of the aisle. Can't you find somewhere else to sit?"

"I'm sorry, sir, but I. . . ."

"Don't you people have any sort of courtesy? You're taking up a lot of room. Why don't you fold that thing up and sit in the seats like the rest of us?"

"I can't. . . ." Sarah's voice quavered.

Suddenly Izzy loomed over the man. He looked furious and formidable in spite of the bright, clownish bow tie. "Apologize, please."

"Huh?" The man looked at him in bleary amazement.

"Apologize to her. She wasn't hurting anything or anyone. You're the one who's drunk and can't walk a straight line."

"Izzy," Gary warned, but it was no use. Besides, if Izzy hadn't said something, Andrew, Josh, or Jake would have. They were all on their feet, fists clenched, jaws tight.

"What's with you kids? I'm just making conversation and you're acting like it's a federal offense." The drunk backed off, hazily aware that he'd overstepped some boundaries.

"Apologize." Izzy's voice was low and frightening, a tone none of the others had ever heard.

"Forget it, Izzy," Sarah murmured softly. "It's okay."

"No it's not. He was rude to you. He should apologize."

"Please don't make a scene," she begged. "*Please.*"

While Izzy was distracted, the older man wisely backed away and disappeared into the crowd.

Izzy sank down on his seat and took Sarah's hands in his own. "Why didn't you let me punch him out?" He sounded disappointed.

"Fists and violence don't do any good, Izz. That 'eye for an eye and tooth for a tooth' stuff went out with the Old Testament. Besides, it's not the first time it's happened—to me *or* to others—and I'm sure it won't be the last. Handicapped people have to get used to a lot of unpleasant stuff. But thanks for sticking up for me. I appreciate it. I really do." She smiled at him gently, with a radiant look on her features that conveyed the inner peace the others couldn't understand. Izzy melted.

Still, the fury they all felt did not go away.

CHAPTER 4

LIVE

FROM BRENTWOOD HIGH

"Let's wait until the crowd thins out," Gary suggested after the play. He glanced covertly at Sarah who was studying the playbill.

"What'd you think, Andrew? Did you like it?"

Andrew wrinkled his nose. "I'm not sure. The main character sure worried a lot about himself—and talked about it too."

"Those are soliloquies," Gary explained. "If you were reading a novel, it would be easy to get inside a character's head and know his thoughts. It's a little harder on stage."

"I liked it," Kate said. "But I wish he'd died at the end."

"Who'd want to sit through a two hour play to see that?" Molly asked. "Kate, you're morbid."

"I agree with Kate," Julie piped. "It would have made the play much more believable."

"Sounds as though you'll have no trouble taking sides for the reviews," Gary said with a chuckle. He looked around at the emptying theater. "I think we can leave now."

Darby pushed Sarah's wheelchair to the top of the stairs.

"Here we go again," Sarah said gamely. "I think it will be worse going down."

"We can take you backward," Andrew offered. "Then you won't have to look."

Sarah nodded and closed her eyes. The boys picked up the chair and started down the steps. Darby, Molly, Julie, and Kate watched. On the third step from the bottom, Jake stumbled. His corner of the chair lurched downward. Sarah gasped and a terrified expression flickered on her face.

Almost as quickly as it had happened, Jake caught himself. With his shoulder, he pressed against the chair. Izzy braced himself against the step, ready to take the full weight of Sarah's chair if necessary.

"Got it," Jake breathed. "Sorry about that, Sarah."

She released a quivering sigh. "It's okay. You just wanted to give me one more thrill tonight, I guess." She passed a hand across her eyes and closed them again.

As she did so, Molly reached out and grabbed Darby's hand. "Did you *see* that? They all could have fallen!"

"I know. My knees are shaking!"

"I never realized until tonight just how dependent Sarah is on others," Molly said. "She does so well in school that I take it for granted that she can do anything."

"It must be awful," Kate agreed. "I'd hate it."

"Me too." It wasn't often that Julie or Kate were

sympathetic to anyone's cause but tonight they were all united in agreement as they watched Izzy push Sarah toward her van.

"No wonder she likes her van so much," Kate continued. "It gives her the kind of freedom we take for granted."

"I don't think I've appreciated Sarah enough," Molly reflected. "She's awesome. She handles her disability without complaining. How does she *do* that?"

––––––––

The after-theater coffee shop was nearly full when they arrived. The walls rang with conversation and laughter. Theater posters covered the walls of the two-level bistro. A huge brass espresso maker took up one entire corner of the coffee bar. Waitresses were scurrying back and forth with steaming mugs of fragrant coffees and plates of biscotti.

Molly and Julie were nearest the reservation podium when the hostess arrived. The woman, her hair a blond tangle, looked harried. She eyed the large group warily.

"What can I do for you?" Her voice was not welcoming. She sounded as though the group had come intentionally to irritate her.

"A table for ten, please."

The hostess tipped her head toward Sarah. "Her too?"

"Of course!"

"We've only got a few places that wheelchairs will fit in here and not get in the way. Besides that, there's only one table in that part of the room that will seat ten and it's full. If you want to split up, I can put her down here and the rest of you on the second level."

"Leave Sarah?" Molly looked dumbfounded. "We can't do that!"

"Suit yourself. It's a busy night. Could be an hour or more before the table will be empty. Try not to stand in the doorway and get in people's way."

"But you can't just leave us standing here," Julie protested.

"Can't help it you brought a wheelchair in here. The tables are full. Like I said, there's probably room on the second level but. . . ."

"Go ahead, please," Sarah said. "Take the table up-stairs. I don't mind waiting. I'm sure it won't be long before a smaller table opens down here."

"And leave you sitting here alone? No way."

"Maybe one of you could keep me company. I don't want all of you standing here because of me." Sarah's gentle eyes were troubled. "I'm serious."

"So are we." Julie took the handles of the wheel-chair and turned Sarah around. "We're leaving. Right, guys?"

"Right."

"Absolutely."

"We're outa here."

En masse the group turned to depart. Sarah's pro-tests were lost in the chatter.

Once out in the street, they regrouped like a flock of angry wet hens.

"Can you believe it? That woman was so *rude*."

"I've never been treated like that before in my life!"

"If my parents had an employee like that at Figaro's," Andrew referred to the posh restaurant his parents owned, "they'd fire her in a minute. No, a second!"

"How could she act that way? Stick Sarah off by herself like she was somebody's in-the-way overshoes instead of a person? I mean, really!"

"Shhhh. Shhhhh. It's okay. It *is*." Sarah's voice finally pierced the babble. "Calm down. This isn't the first time this has happened and it probably won't be the last. The lady was tired, that's all."

"This has happened before?"

"Not exactly, but similar incidents. Not everyone is accommodating to a wheelchair."

"I can't believe it! Why not?"

"First the theater and now this!"

"But those people are in the minority," Sarah continued. "Not everyone is like the woman we saw tonight. Usually people are very nice," her lip quirked in gentle amusement, "unless, of course, they're waiting to get on a busy elevator."

Izzy stood on the sidewalk clenching and unclenching his fists and practically growling with outrage. "I wish I could *do* something."

"First, I think we'd better find a place to sit down," Gary suggested calmly. He'd been silent through all of this, watching the kids' reactions. "There's a little place down the street where I eat sometimes. It's not fashionable or trendy, but it's got tables and chairs and easy access. Come on."

They had to forcibly shove Izzy into a chair at the cafe. He was still fuming impotently about the evening's events. Tactfully, Gary sat down next to him.

"Anger doesn't do much good, Izz-man," he said finally.

"But nobody should get treated like that. Not Sarah! Who's she ever hurt or insulted in her entire life? Nobody, that's who."

"It's not me personally, Izzy. It's the chair. Some people just don't handle it very well."

Izzy looked at Sarah with soft, caring eyes. "I just wish there was some way I could fix what happened to you tonight."

"Maybe there is." Gary's surprising comment got everyone's attention.

"I can't think of anything except going back and telling that lady . . ." Izzy's voice trailed away. The others could practically see a light bulb flickering on inside his head. "Except maybe doing a story on the way the handicapped are treated." He snapped his thick fingers. "That's it! We can do an exposé on how the handicapped are treated! We can show others how it feels to be in a wheelchair."

"How are we supposed to do that?" Kate asked. "Sarah's the only one in a wheelchair."

"True," Josh said softly, "but that doesn't mean we couldn't *pretend* to be handicapped."

Like wildfire, enthusiasm spread through the group.

"We can go undercover! Wheelchairs, white canes, whatever disability we think needs to be investigated. It's the only way we can ever really know how it feels. Besides," and Jake looked at Sarah with a smile, "then we'll be able to understand you better."

Sarah laughed and shook her head. "You guys are too much! Why would anyone choose to be handicapped, even for a day?"

"For a story," Julie said.

"And for a friend," Darby added gently.

"What do you think, Gary?"

He shrugged noncommittally. "Fine with me if Rosie will go for it. I'd like to see you work in pairs. One disabled, the other, his or her companion."

"Sounds fine," Jake said. "We can go to the mall, to restaurants, movie theaters, everywhere normal teenagers want to go. Since most places are already handicapped accessible or at least working in that direction, the focus of our story should be the *personal* aspect. The attitudes of the *people* we run into. Are they courteous and kind? Rude? Difficult? I think it will be a great program to inform and to educate."

"Then Ms. Wright should love it," Kate said. "She's big into that stuff."

"What about filming?" Josh wondered. "If we're supposed to be undercover, how will we get this on tape?"

"Interviews, mostly," Izzy said, "but we could also use one of those small home video cameras for a few shots. They're small and inconspicuous. Even though they don't produce as good a quality picture, it should work. After all, don't undercover investigations break a few rules?"

Gary cleared his throat. "Just so you understand, there will be *no* rule breaking with this project. You can't tape someone and show their faces on television without asking their permission first."

"What if we distort faces and voices?" Izzy asked.

"I'll talk to Rosie about it."

"This is going to be so cool," Julie enthused.

"Ms. Wright will eat this up," Molly chortled.

"Good idea, Izzy," Josh said. Then he turned to Sarah. "What do you think?"

Sarah chewed for a moment on her lower lip. "I don't quite know. It's very sweet of all of you to care so much about my feelings and those of others who are handicapped, but it seems like a very difficult undertaking."

"Is something bothering you, Sarah?" Darby asked.

"Not exactly," Sarah responded, a frown marring her pretty features. "I just hope I haven't inspired something that isn't going to work out."

The group exchanged glances among themselves. This was a big project—and an important one. They wouldn't blow it—would they?

CHAPTER 5

LIVE

FROM BRENTWOOD HIGH

"I think the play reviews turned out really well, don't you?" Molly asked of Darby and Jake as they walked toward the media room.

"Ms. Wright talked to the manager of the theater and he thanked her for the stories. He thought it would actually help ticket sales for the rest of the run. He's offering a student price for matinee tickets next week."

"Awesome." Molly giggled. "I like having so much power. We can actually affect the way people think!"

"Sometimes it's fun," Jake admitted, "but other times I think it's rather frightening."

"You do? Why?"

"Because of the amount of influence broadcast and print media have. I don't feel smart enough or experienced enough to influence people's minds."

"You think too much, Jake," Molly chided, unfazed by his comments. "Don't you agree, Darby?"

They turned into the doorway of Chaos Central and paused. The room was empty but for Sarah. She was seated near the window, silhouetted in light, staring blankly toward the street. Her face, usually so vibrant with expression, was glum.

"Sarah? Are you all right?" Darby moved toward her friend.

Jake and Molly followed. "What's going on?"

Sarah turned her head away. When she finally looked at the threesome, there were tears shining in her eyes.

"What's the matter, hon?" Darby knelt by Sarah's chair and took her hands in her own. "Has something happened?"

"Nothing, really, it's just that. . . ." Sarah's voice snagged. "Never mind."

"Don't even think you can get away with that!" Darby chided. "Spill it. What's wrong?"

Sarah pulled one hand away and scrubbed at the corner of her eye. "I thought everyone would be out of here right now and I'd have some time to think."

"We got out of class to work because the substitute teacher was having study hall."

"I see." Sarah sighed and turned her chair so that she was facing them. She was wearing her hair in the new style Darby had designed for her.

"Well?" Molly put her hands on her hips and tapped her toe against the tile. "Are you going to tell us?"

"It's hard to explain," Sarah murmured. "Something's been troubling me ever since the night we went to the play."

"Don't let the drunk or that hostess get you down," Molly said. "They were total jerks."

"Oh, it's not them. It's ... it's that I feel like a *freak*!"

They were all dumbfounded by Sarah's blurted confession. Jake finally found his voice. "I don't understand."

"The *Live!* staff is doing this exposé on treatment of the handicapped because of me."

"So? You gave us the idea, but hopefully it will help *every* handicapped person—or at least make the rest of us think a little bit before we're rude or thoughtless again."

"I know. Still, it's weird. Ever since we started talking about this project, I've been thinking about my accident. That's something I haven't done in a long time."

"What *about* your accident?"

"Mostly about what I lost as a result of it. All this focus on me and my handicap really put things into new perspective. Until this started, I somehow believed I was still a little . . . normal. Now I realize that I'll *never* be normal. I can't be." She tapped the arm of her chair. "This is in the way."

Sarah's expression was tremulous, as though she were about to cry. "Until now I fantasized that it was possible for me to be a part of the group, to be considered just 'one of the gang.' But this story and the research that's going into it has shown me that my idea is only a fantasy."

Sarah scrubbed away the tears that had gathered on her eyelashes. "This story is a reality check for me. Unfortunately, I'm not crazy about the reality."

"Don't say that!" Darby said. "You've got it all wrong."

"Wrong? Hardly. It's pretty hard to deny being in a wheelchair."

"True, but it doesn't mean there's something wrong with that. Everybody is different in some way or another."

Sarah looked at her friends doubtfully.

"Don't you see?" Molly burst out. "Josh is black. Kate is Chinese. Shane's from a broken home. Andrew's a stuck-up snob. Izzy is a nut. I have a big mouth. You're in a wheelchair. Every single one of us has something that makes us 'different,' but it doesn't make us 'wrong.' " Molly paused. "Except for Izzy, of course."

Sarah couldn't help but laugh. "So you're equating my wheelchair with your 'big mouth'?"

"Something like that. We haven't been fair to you, Sarah. We jumped into this story without asking you how you felt about it, but we did that because *you're one of us*. We assumed you felt like the rest of us. We didn't think about your feelings because we assumed we *knew* them. Can you forgive us?"

"Forgive you?" Sarah's smile lit the room. "That's the nicest thing anyone has said to me in a long time!"

"*Live!* has the opportunity to educate people, to offer them ways in which they can show respect to others who are different from themselves," Jake said. "*You* taught us that, Sarah. We want others to understand too. We never meant to hurt you with this piece. It's more like a tribute to you and to the bravery of people who've had hardship and overcome it."

Sarah brightened even more. "You mean it?"

"You weren't with us when we ran the idea past

Ms. Wright. She was *excited*. She even said it was the best idea yet—and we've done some good shows. In fact . . ."

At that moment, Josh rolled into the room—literally. He was maneuvering a wheelchair. Unfortunately, he wasn't doing a very good job of it. Before anyone could stop him, he crashed into a metal trash can and sent it careening across the room.

"Oops." Josh did a louie in the chair and ended up facing Sarah. "How do you drive one of these things? My arms are already aching and I just took myself down the hall!"

Sarah laughed and flexed the muscles of her right arm. Josh's mouth dropped open at the sight of the firm, rounded muscle in Sarah's slender arm. "I never realized how strong you are!"

"Constant exercise," Sarah said. "In fact, my mom and dad make me open all the tight jar lids and stuck drawers in our house."

"I can see why." Josh ruefully studied his own arms. "Weight training, here I come."

"Where'd you get the wheels?" Jake asked.

"Gary borrowed some equipment from the hospital. There are three chairs. Want one?"

Before Jake could answer, Andrew tapped his way into Chaos Central with a white cane. He was wearing thick dark glasses and a bemused expression. "This is harder than I thought it would be!" he announced to the room in general. "Oww!" His shin struck a file cabinet.

Andrew whipped off the glasses. There was masking tape on the inside to block his vision. He blinked owlishly until he grew accustomed to the light. "Bummer. I'm glad I'm not blind."

"At least you've learned something during this assignment," Rosie Wright commented as she entered the room behind him. "A little gratitude might be refreshing from you, Andrew."

Andrew scowled but didn't answer. The tip of his cane was stuck in a wad of gum at the base of a chair.

"As you can see, Josh and Andrew already have their assignments. Tomorrow is the big day." With characteristic briskness, Ms. Wright gave out the rest of the assignments for Saturday's undercover operation.

"Darby, you and Kate can also be in wheelchairs. Sarah, you too." Ms. Wright smiled when the girls began to giggle. "You expected me to assign you to something else?"

"I thought maybe I could be blind and Andrew could be the one who couldn't walk."

"Good trick if you can manage it," Andrew muttered. He was still cleaning gum off the tip of his cane.

"Molly, Jake, Julie, and Izzy will be your companions. Each of you will work as a pair. . . ." Ms. Wright glanced around the room. "Where *is* Izzy? I want him and Jake to carry the video cameras. They're small enough to put in the pocket of a jacket." She peered around the room again, as if by wishing him present, Izzy would appear.

"Izzy will show up. He always does. He had his Home Living class last hour. He's probably gorging himself on leftovers."

"Andrew, you take this cane."

"Julie suggested that you put a lift in one shoe to make you limp. You'll have Kate's chair to lean on if you get tired. Want to try it?"

"That would hurt."

"That's the idea. No one ever promised that being handicapped would be fun. . . . What happened to you?" Ms. Wright's attention focused on Shane Donahue as he hobbled into the room on crutches, his foot encased in a large cumbersome cast.

Shane dropped heavily into the nearest chair. A wince of pain flickered across his features. Kate and Julie were the first to his side.

"Is it broken?"

"How'd you do it?"

"What happened?" The group clustered around him staring at the big cast.

"Can I sign it?" Molly asked.

"Gotcha!" Shane gave them one of his rare grins. He leaned over and released a piece of tape. The cast opened and clattered to the floor. "It's fake."

"Cool. Where'd you get it?"

"It sure looks real."

"I made it. I know a guy who owns a drugstore and he gave me the stuff. I've been walking around school all morning trying to get used to the crutches." He rubbed his armpits. "Not easy."

"Very ingenious, Shane. I'm impressed." Ms. Wright was practically glowing with pleasure at her battered-looking staff. "How was your reception?"

"The girls were all nice," Shane commented, "but I almost had to beat up a couple guys who tried to kick the crutches out from under me."

"And they didn't know your cast was fake?" Molly gasped.

"I could tell they thought it was funny. Some joke. If my leg *had* been broken, I would probably have fallen and broken something else too." His eyes narrowed to cold slits. "If I hadn't been trying to stay in character, I would have. . . ."

Ms. Wright cleared her throat. "Never mind. I don't think I want to hear what you would have done. It does appear that there's some educating to be done within the walls of Brentwood High."

Shane turned to look at Sarah. "I don't know how you do it," he said. His expression was intense. "I'd be so frustrated that I'd explode every time someone didn't get out of my way or made a stupid remark . . ."

"You'd learn to cope," Sarah assured him. "Or find things that *help* you to manage."

"I can't think of anything that could do that."

"I have a Bible verse that I repeat sometimes when things get tough."

Shane looked startled, as if that were the very *last* thing he'd consider.

Sarah smiled at his expression and continued. "It's from James. 'Whenever you face trials of any kind, consider it nothing but joy because you know that the testing of your faith produces endurance and let endurance have its full effect, so that you may be mature and complete, lacking in nothing.' "

"That helps?"

"Like my dad says, it's easy to be pleasant and uncomplaining in good circumstances," Sarah explained. "But it's not so easy to treat each other well and to have a good attitude when life seems hard or unfair. Dad says that when I can't think of another good thing about my condition, I can always think of it as an 'opportunity for growth.'" She laughed a little. "Believe me, I've had plenty of those!"

Shane nodded solemnly, considering Sarah's words. Ms. Wright cast her eyes toward the door. "We could get onto something else if Izzy would come . . ."

At that moment, Isador burst into the room. His buzz-cut hair looked practically electrified as did the expression on his face. His agitation was almost tangible as he skidded to a stop in front of Ms. Wright.

Izzy had a baby cradled in his arms. The infant, wrapped in a soft blue blanket, lay nestled next to Izzy's broad chest.

"A baby? Izzy, what's going on here?" Ms. Wright demanded.

The girls all pushed forward for a closer look. Even Jake and Josh leaned over to peek at the child.

Molly put a tentative finger beneath the blanket. "That's no baby! That's a doll!"

"Of course it's a doll, you idiot! Why would I have a baby with me in school?"

"You've done weirder things," Molly retorted. "Have you forgotten about that raccoon and science class? Or the—"

Darby took the doll out of Izzy's arms and peeled back the blanket. Inside was a sweet-faced, life-like vinyl doll with pudgy cheeks. "You have good taste in dolls, Izz. She's cute."

"It's a *he*." Izzy scowled. "And don't squeeze him so hard. I don't know what makes him cry."

Shane looked at Izzy as though the larger boy were foaming at the mouth. "When did you start playing with dolls? Is this a recent obsession?"

Anyone but Shane would have backed away from the glare Izzy gave him. "I'm not 'playing' with him. He's my assignment." Izzy glanced at Julie who was now holding the doll. "Watch out! He's delicate!"

"Aren't you awfully attached to this doll, Izzy, for only having it for a few minutes?"

Izzy groaned and ran his thick fingers through the stubble of his hair. "The Home Living unit is studying marriage, pregnancy, child care—that sort of stuff. Our current unit is on teen pregnancies. Everybody in the class got a doll. We're supposed to carry them around and take care of them as if they were real babies for two weeks. That way we actually get an idea of how it might be to be a teenager trying to go to high school and care for a real baby."

"That's a big improvement over the class when I took it last year. We had to carry hard-boiled eggs around and pretend they were babies. I painted a little face and diaper on mine, but it still didn't feel much like a baby," Molly said.

"You dropped it on the floor in the lunchroom," Kate reminded her. "Phew! What a smell!"

"The egg, er, baby, was two weeks old. What'd you expect?"

"I think this baby looks just like you," Josh said, peering into the doll's face. "Chubby cheeks, pug nose . . . what's that?"

Josh jumped backward as the doll started to wail. It was a piercing, annoying cry that sent some scrambling backwards, others forward to see what had happened to the baby.

"That's the microprocessor inside." Izzy grabbed the doll and began to tinker with it. Suddenly, the crying stopped. "Every doll is programmed differently, each to cry at random intervals like a real baby might. It's supposed to mimic a real baby's needs. Some of the dolls are programmed to be 'good' babies, others to be 'colicky.' I don't know which I have yet."

"But how did you get it to stop crying? It sounds so real!"

"That's because it's a recording of a real baby's cry."

Izzy flipped the doll onto its stomach to reveal that he was holding a small key in a slot in the doll's back. "As long as I hold this key in this slot for as long as it takes to feed a baby, the doll will be quiet. If I take it out before the doll's ready to be quiet, it will start to cry again."

"Just put it in the garbage can with a pillow over it," Kate suggested.

"You wouldn't do that to a real baby!" Izzy protested. "Besides, the computer chip records how much time the doll spends crying. It's part of my grade. I can't do that. I have to sit here and hold it."

"Just as though it were a real baby," Ms. Wright concluded. "What a great idea."

"And there's no way to turn it off?"

"If the computer chip indicates tampering, I flunk the class."

"So it actually does act like a real baby!"

Izzy stared at the plastic infant in his hands.

"'Fraid so." He lifted the doll to his face and peered into its eyes. "I think I got one of the colicky ones. That's bad. I'm afraid it's going to keep me up tonight."

"Mooney, if there's a life weirder than yours, I'd like to hear about it," Andrew said. "And put some diapers on that thing. It's disgusting."

Izzy rocked the baby protectively against his chest still holding the key in place. "Lay off. This is just a little kid."

"It's not *real*, Isador."

"If I have to be stuck with this doll for the next two weeks, it's going to seem *very* real to me." Izzy was instinctively cradling the doll in his arms and rocking slightly on the balls of his feet. He'd no doubt held his little sisters in just the same way.

"What about our project? You're one of the companions and you're supposed to run a camera. We can't go without you."

"Leave it in the car," Shane suggested.

"That's child abuse. He can't do that."

"Then how is he supposed to go anywhere in the next two weeks?"

"I can either take it with me or get a baby-sitter. That's one of the rules because that's what I'd have to do with a real baby."

"So get a sitter. Your sisters would love to have the doll."

"They're too young."

"Izzy, it's a *doll*!"

"We have to treat this like a *real* infant. My little sisters would play with it for a while and then leave it lying around. Besides, if I get a baby-sitter, I have to *pay* for it and I don't have any spare cash."

"Why would you have to pay someone to sit with a lump of plastic and a computer chip?"

"The rules...."

"Forget I asked!" Andrew exclaimed.

"Isador, if necessary, we will chip in enough money to hire someone to 'baby-sit' your doll. We need you for this story." Ms. Wright looked half amused, half perturbed.

"How about your grandmother?" Darby suggested. "Wouldn't she like to take care of her ... great-grandchild ... for a few hours?"

"Good idea!" Izzy looked relieved. "Grandma probably wouldn't mind at all. She's the only one who might actually sit and hold the key in this dumb thing's back so it won't cry."

"Don't call your offspring a 'dumb thing,' Izzy. It's a bad reflection on yourself, not to mention not very self-confidence-building for your child." Josh's grin was a mile wide as he spoke.

"At least we have that settled. Izzy will leave the doll with his grandmother while we go undercover. Now we have to discuss when and where we'll meet...."

After Ms. Wright had left the room to run off some copies in the teachers' lounge, the kids from the *Live!* staff remained behind.

"What's going on tonight?" Andrew wondered. "Is anything happening?"

"Friday night in Brentwood. Big deal."

Julie and Kate both smiled smugly. "We've got dates."

"From another school, no doubt," Andrew sneered.

"Don't criticize," Julie warned. "If you had plans for tonight, you wouldn't be asking us what *we're* doing."

"There's a live band at Urban Union tonight. That's usually fun," Jake said. He referred to a new coffee house attracting a lot of recent attention. He glanced at Darby and Molly. "Anybody interested?"

A whimper escaped Izzy as he sat in a chair holding his doll to his chest. He'd tried releasing the silencing key in the doll's back two or three times with no success. Every time he did so, the infant let out an ear-piercing wail.

"Why the long face, Izz-man?" Jake wondered. "You can go too."

"My parents are going out of town for a meeting tonight and Grandma is going to ride with them to visit a friend. They won't be back till late. I'm stuck baby-sitting my little sisters and this stupid doll."

Izzy stared glumly at his friend, his round face creased with worry and his broad shoulders slumped with burden. "Being a father is *tough*!"

CHAPTER 6

LIVE FROM BRENTWOOD HIGH

"You're quiet," Molly observed as she, Darby, and Sarah drove toward Sarah's house to watch some videos Ms. Wright had recommended.

It was true. Though Sarah was never what anyone would call boisterous, she was usually not quite so pensive either.

"Sorry. I've had a lot on my mind."

"Problems?" Molly's expression grew concerned.

"Not really. It's just that a lot has come up lately." Sarah pulled into the driveway and turned off the ignition. "But I'd rather not talk about it. It's nothing."

Molly and Darby exchanged concerned glances as they exited the van.

They were all settled in Sarah's family room before she spoke again. "I didn't mean to be rude earlier. It's just that some things are very difficult to discuss."

"But those are probably the things you *need* to discuss," Darby said pragmatically. "It's the stuff that hurts the most that needs to come out."

"Like a sliver in your finger," Molly added. "Or a stone in the bottom of your shoe."

"Maybe you're right." Sarah cocked her head to

one side and stared out the window. The house was quiet. "It's this dating stuff that's got me down. I've said it before. Everybody seems to have somebody to go out with except me."

"But would you actually change places with me?" Molly wondered. "Andrew Tremaine keeps asking me out and I wonder what I've done wrong to deserve that!"

"You like Andrew a little," Sarah chided softly. "Admit it."

"A little. In the same way I got attached to this ugly blue pillow I have. It's been around so long that I'd miss it if it were gone."

"Besides," Darby added, "Ms. Wright told us at the very beginning that the *Live! From Brentwood High* media room was *not* the place to look for a prom date."

"But we're with those guys more than any others in school."

"Still, we're supposed to be professional at the studio."

"It's easy for you to say, Darby. You've dated other guys, and I see the way Jake looks at you. Julie and Kate are dating all the time. . . ."

Sarah visibly shook herself. "I've never felt so selfish. It's just that I'll be seventeen years old on my next birthday and I've never had a date. I feel left out."

"You aren't the only one. . . ."

Sarah didn't listen. "I've been looking through the Bible for verses on patience, but that doesn't change the fact that everybody seems to have somebody except me."

Darby and Molly were surprised to see tears in Sarah's eyes. "If I'm honest, it's not even the dating and guy thing that's bothering me. It's that I hate feeling so different from everybody else. The story we're working on reminds me over and over again." She curled a fist and pounded it against the arm of her chair. "This thing always gets in the way!"

"But Sarah—"

"It's true, Molly, no matter what you try to say. Look at me! I'm not even on your eye level unless you're sitting down. Do you know how it feels to always be looking at someone's belt buckle instead of their face? Worse yet, sometimes I feel like the chair has a 'don't touch' sign on it. People seldom reach out and touch me. No one puts their arms around me or holds my hand. It feels too awkward to them. I can't blame them, but that doesn't mean I still don't want to be touched. I *need* to be touched."

"Maybe that's what this story will be good for then," Darby finally said, "to teach others how it feels to be handicapped—and how to reach out."

"Maybe. I know this chair intimidates a lot of people. And if someone doesn't know how to approach me, then they'll never really get to know me." Sarah's expression was sad. "I know there's nothing I can do to change it, but it leaves me feeling very empty and alone sometimes."

"You wouldn't even *want* a guy who couldn't get past your chair, Sarah!" Molly said. "Who'd want to date anyone who got hung up on that?"

"But does that sort of guy even exist?" Sarah asked. She rolled her eyes. "Do I sound really selfish? If I do, I'm sorry."

"You don't sound selfish at all. You sound perfectly normal," Darby said. "All girls worry about guys. You'd be abnormal if you didn't. Plus, I don't think you should worry about the chair anymore. It might have taken Molly and me a little longer to get to know you because we didn't quite know how to get around the wheelchair, but believe me, the effort was worth it."

Darby reached out and put her hand on Sarah's arm. "And the right guy is going to feel exactly the same way."

Sarah's bright smile lit the room. "The best thing about *Live!* is the people I've met. Thank you."

Darby chewed on her lower lip, deep in thought. "I know this would be hard for you, Sarah, but I wish you'd let someone interview you for the show. It would be perfect if you'd talk to the camera like you've been talking to us. Let people know how you feel. That way, our viewers will know how important it is to look past the chair to the person in it."

"I don't know. . . ."

"You're the best person for the interview. You've already thought all of this through. You've discussed it with us. You know what you need to say."

"Maybe others think differently."

"Then we'll interview others too. What do you think?"

"I think I feel like a crybaby and a whiner!"

"You? Are you kidding?"

"I don't want anyone to feel sorry for me. Pity is

the last thing I want. In fact, I haven't enjoyed this pity party I've been having for myself at all. It's stopping right now." Sarah looked determined.

"Then you'll do it. The interview will be a way of educating people, not a 'whining' session."

"I agree with Darby," Molly said. "Until people understand how it feels to be in a wheelchair or on crutches, they'll continue to be put off by disabilities. Everybody's got a handicap—in this case, lack of knowledge!"

"If sharing my story would do that, it might be worth it."

"That's the right spirit!"

Sarah became visibly more cheerful. Her shoulders straightened and her eyes twinkled. "I have to say thanks to you two."

"What for? Hassling you? Giving you a major lecture?"

"No. For reminding me that maybe I do have a purpose in life—one I hadn't considered until now. I've always wondered *why* this happened to me. Maybe part of the answer is that I should be helping take the mystery out of being handicapped, helping the non-handicapped to realize that we're all the same in our emotions, our wishes, and our dreams. I *like* the idea of helping others. If sharing my story would do that, then it's worth it."

A shadow flickered across her features.

"What's wrong?" Darby wondered.

"That's still not going to fix the 'guy problem.' Maybe I'd better get used to the idea that I'll never find a guy mature enough to overlook my wheelchair."

Then Sarah smiled that radiant smile she had. "I guess I'll just have to listen to my mom's advice."

"What's that?"

"That the picking of life partners should be left to God. After all, He's the one who knows what's best for me. My mom and dad both prayed that God would pick out a mate for them and they found each other. They're very happy together."

" 'Handpicked by God,' " Molly murmured. "Wow. What a great concept."

A sly expression crossed Molly's features. "Even if you let God pick a guy for you, I'm still curious. Who do *you* like?"

Much to both Molly's and Darby's surprise, Sarah blushed a furious pink.

"So there *is* someone special! Who?"

"I can't say."

"You mean you *won't* say." Molly wagged a finger in Sarah's face. "Don't worry. Once he—whoever he is—gets to know you, he'd have to be crazy not to like you."

The clock on the mantel chimed and Darby jumped to her feet. "We'd better go. Hang in there, Sarah. It's going to work out for you. I just know it."

Molly and Darby were thoughtful as they walked toward the bus stop.

"I wish Sarah could meet a really great guy," Darby said with a sigh. "Someone as kind and considerate as she is should have the very best."

"Is there any way *we* could help?" Molly wondered. Then she rolled her eyes. "But what am I saying? I can't even help myself. *Andrew* wants me to go out with him again this weekend!"

"We could have a party," Darby suggested. "It would be a way to introduce Sarah to some people outside the *Live!* staff. Besides, we haven't done anything fun lately."

"What a great idea!" Molly skipped a step and her curls bounced. "We can have it at my house. You and I can plan the food. Chips and salsa, pizza, submarine sandwiches . . . and people! Let's make out a list. . . ."

Cars began to converge on the mall at 11:00 Saturday morning. The undercover investigation was about to begin.

Darby and Molly had come with Sarah who had the extra wheelchairs in her van. Izzy, Jake, Josh, Andrew, and Shane arrived together, followed closely by Julie and Kate. Ms. Wright and Gary Richmond pulled up in Gary's ancient and disreputable car.

"Won't people think it's funny to see you pull your wheelchair out of the van and then sit down in it?" Molly wondered.

"I'll park so that the door is next to Gary's car. That will conceal what we're doing."

"I feel so sneaky," Molly muttered. "Are you sure this isn't dishonest?"

"This is *research*. Besides, it's not hurting anyone. The only people who could possibly be embarrassed by what we're doing are those who intentionally harass or are rude to the handicapped."

Jake opened the back door of the van to remove the extra wheelchairs.

"Are you ready for this?" Darby asked with a smile.

Jake rolled his eyes. "I thought so, until I saw Izzy."

"Oh, oh. What's that supposed to mean?"

"He's really into this undercover thing."

"That's not so bad," Sarah said.

"No, but the fact that he decided to bring his doll with him is pretty awful."

"You're kidding! Aren't you?"

"I wish I were. Wait till you see him. He's got some sort of harness hooked up under his coat so that he can put the camera there. That way his hands will be free to push the stroller."

Just then Izzy appeared, wearing a bulky jacket and pushing a stroller and what appeared to be a baby smothered in blankets.

"Are you planning to push that baby to the Arctic Circle? You've got enough covers over it!"

"I didn't want anyone to be able to peek in and see that it was just a doll. They'd think I was weird."

"Too late," Andrew said. "You're already weird."

"Why didn't you leave it at home with your family or get a sitter?"

"It didn't work out. Besides, the more I thought about it, the more I realized that no one but me will probably take its crying seriously and hold the key in its back the entire time. I don't want to get a crummy grade in Home Living because someone else gets careless. I have a four-point grade average to consider, you know. Besides, I just bought more memory for my computer and I'm out of money."

"There's no way you can push that thing and work the camera, Izzy. We need *decent* film footage. You know that. Besides, who's going to push my wheelchair and be my companion if you're messing with that thing?" Josh sounded exasperated.

"Then *you* carry the doll." Izzy picked up the baby and thrust it into Josh's arms. "Be careful you don't turn it upside down or anything."

Josh looked at the thing in his arms with horror. He thrust it out to arm's length. "Oh no. No way. Uh-uh. I'm not riding around in a wheelchair carrying *that!*"

"Then what am I supposed to do?" Izzy growled.

"I don't mind carrying the doll," Sarah offered softly. "It's kind of cute."

"You would?" Izzy looked hopeful. "That would be great! You'd be careful with it too, not like Josh. He'd be likely to dump it in a fountain somewhere."

"Sarah, you have saved my life. I am totally grateful to you for this." Josh looked even more relieved than Izzy. "If I'd had to carry that. . . ."

Izzy plucked the doll out of Josh's grip and gently laid it in Sarah's open arms. "Then I'll be your companion and Molly can go with Josh. If it starts to cry, I'll have to show you what to do." He tucked the baby blankets around the doll as he spoke.

Julie burst out laughing.

"What's so funny?" Izzy glared at her. "If it's this doll thing, get over it!"

"It's just that you look like a . . . family!"

It was true.

Sarah blushed furiously at Julie's observation.

Izzy turned red to the roots of his hair.

"Could this be like an omen or something?" Julie persisted. "You two are perfect together!"

Fortunately for Izzy and Sarah, there was no time for speculation. Ms. Wright sailed up at that moment and began giving orders.

"Molly, you go with Josh. Jake, you take Darby. Julie, that leaves you for Kate. Shane, quit doing acrobatics on your crutches. Andrew, quit poking people with that cane!"

"Don't worry, we'll behave once we get inside."

"You can't break character, not even once. Take a minute to quiet yourselves and to remember what you are. Believe that those chairs and crutches and cane are realities for you. It's not so funny when, after today, you can't get up and walk. . . ."

"She's right about that," Sarah said softly. Her words had a sobering effect on the group. Their playful antics ground to a halt. Shane sank heavily onto the arm pieces of his crutches and his knuckles whitened around the handgrips. He really did appear to need the crutches to walk.

Quietly Andrew slipped his dark glasses into place. For once, there was no sneer on his features, only a thoughtful, almost sad expression. It was apparent that he was truly imagining what it might be like to be blind.

Though Kate could not quit staring at Sarah, Josh was the one who spoke the words they were all thinking.

"Until this minute I didn't take this very seriously." He tapped the arm of the chair. "But I'd hate to be in it for the rest of my life. I'm sorry if I've ever made any stupid jokes, Sarah, about your being lucky to get to ride around instead of walk. I'm very thankful that when we're done with this assignment I'll be able to get up and walk away from this chair—and I'm sorry you can't."

They were all silent. Sarah smiled tremulously at first and then with such sweetness that it lit her face. "Thank you, Josh, but don't worry. I think it's wonderful of all of you to take a walk in *my* shoes. Not every 'normal' teenager would bother. If this story helps anyone to be a little kinder or more compassionate or patient with someone who's moving too slowly in the fast lane, then this is all worth it."

Then Sarah honked the little toy horn she had hidden in the seat of her chair. "So what are we waiting for? Let's go!"

"Everybody take a different level and wing of the mall!" Ms. Wright instructed. "Go to as many stores as you can in four hours. "You should all go out to eat—pick your favorite restaurants and see how they're set up for the handicapped. Also, as we discussed in class, you should each attempt to buy an item of clothing that you must try on and ask to see something from a rack that is over your head. Also ask questions about a specific item, a radio, a model kit, jewelry, whatever. Be real shoppers."

"What if I have to go to the bathroom?" Josh wondered nervously. He glanced at Molly. "She won't be any help."

"Then you'll have to manage on your own. In fact,

I think all of you should use the rest rooms. That will be a learning experience."

"Maybe *you* want to ride in the chair, Molly," Josh offered. The implications of what they were about to do had begun to sink in.

"Thanks but no thanks." Molly grinned impishly. "I'll leave that to you."

"Again, I remind you. Do not break character. For the next four hours, you *are* wheelchair bound. You *are* blind or on crutches."

"But if Molly can't help Josh into the bathroom, then I can't help Sarah either," Izzy fumed. "What's she supposed to—"

"Don't worry about me, Izz," Sarah's laughter filtered across the parking lot. "Remember? I'm the one with experience here!"

Ms. Wright turned to Sarah, her expression thoughtful. "We could have just asked you to do this story, couldn't we?"

"Yes, but I'm glad you didn't. It's kind of nice to have some wheelchair 'buddies' for a day."

Ms. Wright nodded. "You've felt very alone, haven't you?"

Sarah's eyes were bright with unshed tears, but her words were upbeat and cheerful. "I have—until today." She looked across the crazy crew gathered around her. Jake was wearing a truly ugly baseball cap sideways on his head. Izzy was fussing with the doll's wad of blankets. Shane was swinging on his crutches like a demented monkey. "But today is going to be special!"

"Okay, then, let's roll. Report back to me at the

main entry of the mall in four hours."

Like runaway cars they spread out across the parking lot heading for the large front doors of the mall.

"Do you think this is going to work?" Gary asked just before Darby and Jake were out of earshot.

Jake turned back, twisted the bill of his cap to the front of his head and tugged it down tight. "You bet! If we can't open a few eyes and a few minds with this story, then you can fire us all from the *Live!* staff." Jake's smile faded. "And I don't think there's one of us who wants that to happen!"

CHAPTER 8

LIVE

FROM BRENTWOOD HIGH

"Don't push me so fast!" Kate said as Julie wheeled her down the middle aisle of the mall. "I want to look in the windows."

"You can look tomorrow."

"We're supposed to spend four hours here *today*. What's wrong with looking now? There's a great pair of jeans in Maury's window. Wheel me over there."

"Kate . . ." Julie said through gritted teeth.

"What?"

"There's a bunch of little kids staring at us."

"So?"

"I don't like it. They're looking at us like we're freaks!"

"They can't know what we're doing," Kate said. "It just must be the chair. Dumb kids. Haven't they seen a wheelchair before?" She turned to look at the cluster of young boys staring intently at them. "Ignore them."

Kate tipped her nose in the air and turned her head away. While Julie made an awkward attempt at turning the chair toward the door of the store, the boys moved closer.

The oldest, the obvious ring leader, hooked his thumbs in the front pockets of his jeans, and pinioned Kate with his gaze.

"What happened to you?" he asked.

"What business is it of yours?" Kate snapped.

"Just wondered. Were you, like, in a car accident or something?"

"Or something."

The boy would not be deterred. "Is it weird to be crippled?"

Kate swallowed thickly and looked at Julie as if to say "Now what?"

"Listen, we'd love to stay and chat," Julie said, "but we're shopping, so if you'll excuse us. . . ." With an heroic thrust, she catapulted Kate toward the store, leaving the staring boys behind.

"That was strange," Kate muttered once they were safely inside. "What did they think I was? Public property? An animal in a zoo?" She shuddered. "I don't like being noticed like that."

"But that's what the chair does," Julie concluded. "It makes you different than you were before." She picked up a blouse and stared at it unseeing. "Poor Sarah."

"Maybe those kids weren't so bad," Kate muttered. "At least they asked questions. I think it might have been even more uncomfortable if they'd just stood and stared. Maybe I should have been nicer to them. . . ."

"May I help you?" The sales clerk had come up behind them so silently that neither had heard her.

"I'd like to try on some clothes," Kate said.

"Shirts, jeans, maybe something dressy." She held up the blouse. "This, for instance."

They moved slowly through the store picking up the items Kate wanted to try on. Several times Julie and Kate had to pause while other shoppers got out of their way.

"I'm sorry the aisles are so narrow," the clerk apologized. "It seems every time we turn around someone has added another rack or display case. I know it's not easy to navigate through here. We do have a handicapped accessible dressing room, however. It's right this way."

Julie rolled Kate into the cubicle. It was just large enough for her to get the chair turned around. "They don't give you any extra space do they?" she observed.

Kate hopped out of the chair and began to try on clothes. "No. If I had to *stay* in that chair to do this, I'd be tied into a knot. How do you like this shirt?" She pirouetted in front of the mirror.

Just then there was a knock at the door. Kate bolted back into the wheelchair.

"Do you need any other sizes?" the clerk asked.

"No. Everything is fine."

After the woman left, Kate rolled her eyes. "That was close! What if she'd opened the door?"

"Maybe Ms. Wright was correct. Maybe you should stay in character *all* the time."

"How am I supposed to try clothes on while I'm in a wheelchair? That's so awkward ... but that's the point, isn't it? No one could understand *how* awkward unless they'd tried it—or lived it."

Kate and Julie were subdued as they left the store. They meandered down the hallway until they came to a large toy store.

"Let's go in here," Kate instructed. "I need a birthday gift for my cousin. Maybe I can find something."

"Watch out," Julie advised. "There are a lot of boxes jutting out into the walkways."

Kate tipped her head back and looked upward. Brightly colored boxes of toys were stacked to the ceiling, looming over her. "This place gives me the creeps! I feel like all those boxes are going to come tumbling down on me. It's weird, but you get a different perspective from inside this chair. I feel so . . . *small*."

Julie stopped pushing. "Here's that new game everybody is talking about at school. I want to take a look at it."

As Julie turned away, a woman came down the aisle behind them. Suddenly Kate felt herself being moved. "What's going on?"

"Oh, sorry. I just moved your chair a little bit," the woman responded. "I need to get to these boxes."

"You wouldn't have pushed away a person who was *standing* there, would you?"

"Of course not, but—"

"Then please don't touch my chair again. It's just like shoving me away."

"I'm sorry. I wasn't thinking." The woman grabbed the item she wanted and hurried away.

Julie peered down at Kate. "Are you all right?"

Kate wiped away a tear. "I don't know. I know that

lady didn't mean any harm, but it felt so awful to be shoved aside like that. Why is it that when someone is sitting in a wheelchair, people feel they can treat them differently than when they aren't? More than once already, people have talked to me in this really loud voice—as though because I'm sitting in a wheelchair my hearing has gone bad!"

Kate's expression was troubled. "This is all more complicated than I expected it to be."

———

"I'd like to look at that sports bag," Darby said, pointing to one hanging on the top row next to the ceiling.

"I'll have to get a hook to get it down." The clerk looked nervous as she stretched for the bag. It came swinging down more quickly than Darby had expected. She leaned to the side just as it swung by her head.

"I'm so sorry! I should have had you move, but with the wheelchair and all. . . ."

"It's okay." Darby looked over the bag. "I don't think this is exactly what I want. I would like to try on some shoes, though. The blue and white ones on the front rack." She named a brand name. "Size 7, please."

The clerk looked doubtfully at Darby's feet. Still carrying the sports bag, she walked toward the back room. When she returned, she was holding a shoe box. She pulled a small stool toward Darby and sat down. Her hands fluttered helplessly for a moment over

Darby's loafer-clad feet, obviously fearful of touching or hurting Darby.

Darby waited.

"Do you mind if I take off your shoe?"

"That's the easiest way to try other shoes on," Darby said with a smile.

Cautiously the clerk removed Darby's shoe and replaced it with the new sneaker. Darby lifted her foot to examine the results.

"You can move it!" the woman observed.

Darby allowed her leg to fall back to the footplate with Ms. Wright's admonishment ringing in her ears. *Stay in character.*

Darby purchased the shoes and they got out of the store without further incident.

"Nice wheels!" Jake and Darby turned to see who was talking. A young man in a motorized wheelchair had moved up behind them.

Darby laughed. "Not like yours! How fast can you go in that thing?"

The young man grinned. "Nine miles an hour, tops. What I really want is a. . . ." He uttered a brand name neither Darby or Jake had ever heard. "You know, it's great for sports."

"Sports?" Jake echoed. He looked confused.

"Basketball, racing, you know."

"Oh, yeah, sure." It was obvious Jake had never imagined that someone in a wheelchair would like sports.

"Do you do any of that?" Darby wondered, intrigued.

"Some, but I need a different chair. I'm getting one

soon. I'm already signed up to be on a basketball league at the YMCA. I've been practicing my shooting at home in the driveway. Racing doesn't hold much interest for me right now, but maybe someday."

The gregarious young man might have kept talking, but a pretty girl in jeans and a sweatshirt came hurrying out of a nearby store. "There you are! I thought I'd lost you."

"I decided I'd better get out. A lady in there kept giving me the evil eye. She thought I was going to bump into something with my chair."

With that, he took the girl's hand and they moved away down the hall, holding hands.

"Wow," Jake muttered.

" 'Wow' what?" Darby asked.

"That guy plays basketball, has a girlfriend—all the regular guy stuff. I never realized. . . ." He paused. "I guess I really *did* think that handicapped people were different from me and just didn't accept it until now."

"No wonder Sarah gets frustrated," Darby said. "She's 'normal' too. It would be great to see her going down the hall holding hands with a guy, wouldn't it?"

"It would take a pretty smart guy," Jake said frankly. "Someone who could see past the wheelchair. Until just now I thought I was doing that, but instead I've had my own preconceived notions of what handicapped people can or can't do."

"I'm thirsty," Darby said after they'd walked a little farther. "Want to go to the Food Court and get a lemonade?"

They were maneuvering through the congested

aisle in front of the fast food restaurants when Darby felt a rough bump against her shoulder. The wheelchair tipped slightly and Jake quickly righted it.

"Watch where you're going," a heavy-set boy in jeans and a white T-shirt growled. "You're taking up too much room. Move over."

Startled, Darby stared at him and his companion. He was acting as though the incident were *her* fault!

"I wish they'd make some kind of rule," the fellow was saying. "People who come here with baby strollers and wheelchairs take up too much room. Who do they think they are, anyway? You don't even see 'em until you stumble over them."

The pair sauntered on, oblivious to the glares Darby and Jake were sending their way.

"They acted like I wasn't even here!" Darby yelped. "People forget I'm down here until they run into me. What am I, *invisible*?"

"Calm down," Jake advised. "He's a jerk, that's all."

"Well, there's a world full of them! How inconsiderate! Why shouldn't people in wheelchairs have the same rights as everyone else to be where they please? And so what if a wheelchair takes up a little extra room. People don't *choose* to be in one!"

"Chill out, Darb. He's gone."

Darby drew a deep breath and settled into her chair. Inside, she was still seething.

———

"We'd like a table for two, please," Molly said sweetly.

The waitress looked from Molly to Josh and back again.

"There are only a couple tables out front that will be easy to get to. Is that all right?"

Molly wrinkled her nose. She really wanted to sit in the back of the cafe where the big screen television played, but it hardly seemed worth the effort to make a fuss. "I suppose."

"Maybe we should just skip the food," Josh suggested. "I don't like this very much," he whispered to Molly.

"Let's go to the '50s Cafe," Molly suggested. "That's a cafeteria and there's plenty of room."

She didn't give Josh a choice, but pushed him to the popular dining spot. "Look, we're in luck. No line."

Their "luck," however, was not what Molly had hoped it would be. She pushed Josh to the head of the line and handed him a tray. "Now then, what do you want to eat?"

Josh lifted himself in the chair. "I can't see. What's in the back?"

"Salads mostly. Potato. Macaroni. Rice. Should I push you right to entrees?"

"How do they expect me to help myself?" Josh wondered. "I can't see what I'm supposed to be eating, balance the tray and the plates and move my chair at the same time."

"I'll push you."

"But what if I were alone."

"Hmmm. I see your problem."

"And the dessert bar is on the other side of the

room! I can't be running back and forth. Once I get settled at a table I think I'll have to stay there. This is not very convenient."

"Suddenly everything looks different," Molly admitted. "Maybe we don't want to eat here either. Are you hungry for yogurt?"

After they'd escaped the restaurant, Molly headed straight for the yogurt bar.

"I feel like everywhere I go I'm in the way," Josh complained. He took a bite out of the yogurt cup Molly had handed him. "Worse yet, I'd starve out here if I were in a wheelchair. I can't even get close to most of the food to see what it looks like."

They strolled up and down the halls of the mall for some time before Molly stopped in front of a gift shop full of blown glass figurines.

"My mom's birthday is coming soon. She collects these things. Do you mind if we go in and get her something? She likes glass animals the best." Without waiting for an answer, she pushed Josh through the doors of the store.

The store was empty except for two clerks standing near the cash register. Their heads came up when Molly and Josh entered. Almost as quickly, their heads went down again and they engaged in a spirited discussion.

"They don't want us in here," Josh hissed.

"Why? I'm going to buy something."

"Look around! This place has more glass in it than a window factory. What if my chair bumps into something? We could take down a thousand dollars worth of knick-knacks. Oh, oh, here they come."

The two clerks descended on Molly and Josh like planes landing.

"May we help you?"

"Can we show you something?"

"Is there anything we can *hold* for you?"

Molly cleared her throat. "Do you have any horse figurines? Small ones?"

"If you'll stay there, we'll bring them to you."

"That's all right. We'll just follow you to the display."

One of the clerks stopped short. "It would be difficult to navigate through the aisles. It might be better if we brought the horses to you."

"Oh, it's okay," Molly persisted, determined now to see how these ladies would act.

The older of the two blushed. "It would be a shame to bump into something. We have a very nice selection. I'll just bring a few—"

"If we can't look for ourselves then I'm not interested," Molly said indignantly. "I can shop somewhere else where the aisles are larger." She jerked on Josh's chair so that he nearly fell forward as she pulled him out of the store.

"Temper, temper," he chided.

"They didn't want you in that store! Couldn't you tell?"

"Of course I could. But they couldn't have stopped us if we'd really wanted to go to the back."

"They intimidated us into stopping though. I'm never going to buy another figurine in that store! Their aisles should be wide enough so that anyone can get through without being afraid of doing damage."

Molly scrunched her face into a frown. "Some of the people we've met today have been great. Others. . . ."

"But most people just ignore us—until they think we aren't looking. I can feel eyes staring at the back of my head after we go by."

Molly paused by the drinking fountain. "I'm thirsty."

"Me too." Josh started to get up and then halted. "I guess I'd better not stand up and blow my cover. Is there a paper cup dispenser nearby?"

"Sorry. Guess you'll just have to be thirsty." Molly bent over to take a sip of water.

Just as she did so, a little boy came running by and gave Josh's wheelchair a shove. The child giggled and disappeared into the crowd.

Molly looked up and grabbed for the handgrips before Josh rolled into the wall. Then she put a restraining hand on his shoulder.

"Let me get up and deck that kid," Josh growled.

"That will be great research. How are we going to explain to Ms. Wright that you didn't stay in character—or that you punched out a five-year-old? Besides, you've never punched anyone in your life! Why do you want to start now?"

Josh clenched and unclenched his fists as he considered the question. "It's weird, but just being in this chair makes me feel frustrated. There's more I want to be doing and being. . . ." He looked up at Molly with cloudy eyes. "We aren't just going to be educating others with this story. I think the biggest education is for ourselves!"

CHAPTER 9

LIVE
FROM BRENTWOOD HIGH

"Excuse me, sir, I'd like to know the price of this. . . ." Sarah began.

"I'll be with you in a minute."

Izzy gave an exasperated sigh. They'd been waiting for assistance in the appliance department for over fifteen minutes. "He's helped two people and taken three telephone calls since we came. Do you think it's because one of us is in a wheelchair?"

"I think it's because we're teenagers and he doesn't expect to make a sale," Sarah said. "You can't blame every single bad thing that happens to you on the fact that you're wheelchair bound."

"Fine, but we don't have to take this. We'll go someplace else to buy our *six hundred dollar stereo unit.*" Izzy said the last words loudly. The man looked up from the phone and opened his mouth as though he were about to say something.

Izzy turned his back and walked away.

"We weren't going to buy a stereo! We were going to buy a cord to put on your stereo," Sarah chastised.

"He doesn't need to know that. He lost the sale, that's all. Still," and Izzy grinned, "I'm glad he treated us that way because he's a jerk and not because he had some big prejudice against people in wheelchairs."

"Izzy, you're too much. Do you know that?"

"I've been told. How's my baby doing?"

Sarah adjusted the blankets around the doll. "Fine. Not a peep out of her . . . him . . . it."

"I think we should name it. That would be easier. How about Rufus?"

Sarah wrinkled her nose. "Too ugly. What do you think of Merlin?"

"Not much. How about Edgar?" Izzy looked pleased with the name.

"Oscar?"

"Maybe Wilbur?"

"Gordo?"

"Too wimpy. Maybe we should just call it 'Junior,' after me."

"Good idea, Izz." Sarah patted the doll's back. "Isador Eugene Mooney Junior. It has style."

Just then a little boy, not more than three or four and carrying a stick of pink cotton candy walked up to Sarah. "Hi."

"Hi yourself." Sarah's eyes crinkled at the corners as she looked at the child's sticky cheeks.

"What are you doing in there?" the little boy wondered. He put a tentative toe out to touch the wheelchair.

"I can't walk, so this is how I get around."

"Why?"

"Because I was in an accident and hurt my legs." Sarah was sweet and patient and not the least bit bothered by the child's questions.

"Oh." He studied the chair a moment more and then thrust the cotton candy near to Sarah's face. "Wanna bite?"

"Sammy, don't bother the lady!" Sammy's mother descended on him and grabbed a sticky hand. "I'm sorry. He's so curious that he just goes up to anyone and asks a dozen questions."

"That's all right," Sarah said. "I like people who ask questions. I'd much rather have someone come up and talk to me than to stand back and stare."

After Sammy and his mother had left, Izzy studied Sarah. "You were really nice to that little boy."

"He was sweet."

"And you don't mind when people are curious?"

"*I'm* curious when I see someone in a wheelchair. I wonder what happened to them. It's perfectly natural."

"Then what *does* bother you?"

Sarah chewed thoughtfully on her lip for a moment before answering. "This might sound funny, but I don't like people touching my wheelchair."

Izzy's hand left the back of her chair as though the handgrips had turned white hot.

"Not *you*, silly! Strangers. People I don't know. Those who come up and try to move me or to touch my backpack. I think I don't like it because my chair is an extension of *me*. I don't want to be touched by strangers and therefore I don't like my chair to be handled either. Weird, huh?"

"Makes sense to me. But are you *sure* you don't mind if I—"

"Don't be silly, Izz."

"Okay." He took the handgrips and pushed her into a store.

"Maybe we shouldn't go in here," Sarah suggested. "There's thick carpeting on the floor and it will be harder for you to push me."

"It is tougher, but I don't mind. How do you do it when you're wheeling yourself?"

"I try to avoid carpet. If I can't, I just use an extra push." She flexed her hands. "I'm pretty strong, you know."

"You're practically awesome. I'll bet you could bench press at least—" Izzy's speculation was suddenly cut short.

With a sound which seemed more like that of an air raid siren than an infant, the doll in Sarah's lap erupted into a wail.

"Izzy, what do I do?" Heartbreaking cries came through the blankets. Instinctively Sarah picked up the doll and held it to her chest.

"There's a key you stick in a slot in its back. I've got it right here. . . ." Izzy searched his jeans pockets to no avail. "I *had* it here when I left. I know I did. I changed jeans and I . . . maybe I left it in the pocket of my other pants!" He flailed his hands over his clothing wildly searching.

Sarah tried to muffle the cries by holding the doll face down against her chest but it didn't work. They were attracting attention.

"Where *is* it?" Izzy yelled.

Thinking quickly, Sarah began to rock the doll and sing softly to it as though it were a real baby. "If you'll quit making a spectacle of yourself," she suggested under her breath, "no one will realize this isn't a real child."

"But I had it here. I know I did." Still Izzy calmed down. "I put it right . . . here." He pulled a flat key out of the first pocket he'd searched. Quickly he lifted the blanket and stuck the key into the doll's back and turned it. The cries stopped.

"Now you'll have to hold the key in place until the doll is done crying."

"How long will that be?"

"I don't know. It's one of the fussy babies and it's been quiet a long time. Could be five minutes or half an hour."

"Are you sure you shouldn't have left this thing at home?" Sarah asked, amused and perplexed.

"Leave Junior behind? Sarah, I'm disappointed in you! We're doing some father and plastic son bonding."

"Then start pushing. I hear infants sleep better when they can feel motion."

It took nearly an hour for the doll's cries to run their course. Every few minutes Sarah would try to release the key and the wails would resume. Finally, however, when she took her hand off the key, the doll was silent.

"If this were a real baby I'd be crazy by now," she observed. "Imagine trying to calm a crying infant for that long!"

"This class is supposed to make us aware of the difficulties of teenage parenthood. What it's doing is convincing me that I never want children!"

Izzy glanced around the mall. They were in the center atrium. "I haven't been doing any taping. Wouldn't have worked over Junior's noise. Maybe I should set up here in the middle of the mall and do a 'roving reporter' sort of thing. I've got a tripod in the car."

"Go ahead. Junior and I will sit here and watch. I'm exhausted from all that crying."

Izzy gave Sarah a lop-sided smile and lumbered off to get the tripod.

When Jake and Darby came by thirty minutes later, Izzy was already deep into interviews. He'd hooked a mike into the camera and was intently interviewing anyone who would talk to him. Fortunately, Izzy's wacky charm usually invited conversation, even from strangers.

"Could you tell me, sir, your first response to seeing someone in a wheelchair?"

Izzy had cornered a middle-aged man in a business suit who looked as though he were in a hurry.

"No reponse, really. Maybe curiosity. I might wonder what put them there. I don't know what else— sympathy, maybe."

"Sympathy? Do you mean like pity?"

"They're not the same thing," the man said indignantly. "I think you can have sympathy for a person without pitying them. I broke my leg once in six places. I sat in a wheelchair for three months. I didn't need anyone feeling sorry for me, but I did appreciate it when someone was considerate of my extra needs."

"Thank you, sir, for that insight." Izzy clicked off

the camera when he saw Darby and Jake. "How's it going?"

"We're tired. Most everybody's been very nice but the few who haven't have been horrible. Have you talked to anybody else?"

"Andrew and Shane came by about ten minutes ago. Andrew's got the backsides of his dark glasses painted black so he really can't see much. He got mixed up and almost went into the ladies restroom. It was a good thing Shane stopped him." Izzy grinned wickedly. "Shane was tempted to just let him go in, but he was afraid Andrew would pound him with his cane."

"I'm not sure everyone is cut out for undercover work," Jake observed.

"Are you getting tired?"

They turned around to see Ms. Wright and Gary.

"A little. This is harder than I'd expected."

"Time for a break then. Everyone should be here in a few minutes. Izzy, how many interviews did you get?"

"Ten."

"That should be enough to choose from. When you're all together, come over to my house and we'll do a recap of the day. I'll grill hot dogs and burgers for you as a reward for your hard work." She gave her address.

"Sounds great!"

"See you later."

After they'd gone, Jake poked Darby in the shoulder. "Now that we're officially done with our investigation, do you want to switch places with me? I need to sit down."

Darby was out of the wheelchair like a shot. A flood of relief spread through her as she stood and stretched. She felt very, very lucky. Not everyone could be free of a wheelchair so easily.

CHAPTER 10

LIVE

FROM BRENTWOOD HIGH

Rosie Wright's home was a condominium not far from the mall. It was sleek, white, and contemporary with unique and colorful paintings, sculptures and collages, exactly the kind of house her students expected it would be.

"This is great," Izzy observed of a large piece of cast bronze in the foyer. "What is it?"

"It's called 'Man in the Rain.' Do you like it?"

Izzy twisted his head so that it rested on his shoulder. He squinted and stared at the form. "I don't get it. It doesn't look like a man and I don't see any rain."

Ms. Wright chuckled. "One of these days we'll do a feature on modern sculpture and you can interview the artist. He's from Brentwood."

"Cool." Izzy meandered into the all-white living room and flung himself onto an impossibly large sectional. "Until then I'll just enjoy the 'Elvis on Velvet' hanging in my room."

Shane walked into the room behind Izzy and dropped onto a toadstool-like footstool. "I am whipped. Those crutches were fun at first, but now my armpits feel raw. Worse yet, my wrists are killing me."

"At least you aren't going to be black and blue tomorrow," Andrew retorted. "I must have bumped into every planter and display rack in the mall. My shins feel like they've been at target practice—as targets."

"The last time I was this tired I'd mowed and raked six lawns," Josh admitted.

"Why is everyone so exhausted?" Ms. Wright wondered.

"Part of it is the strain," Darby said. "I kept worrying that I'd be 'found out.' Plus, being handicapped isn't easy. Everything seemed twice as hard when it had to be done from a wheelchair."

"Someone talked to me like I was a little kid," Kate added indignantly. "Don't they know that just because something is wrong with a person's legs it doesn't affect their hearing or their brain?"

"I know *I'm* going to be different around handicapped people from now on. No staring, no ignoring, no pretending I don't see them. I'm going to smile and say 'hi' and act like they're real people. And I'm going to make sure I say something to people who think it's not necessary to make things handicapped accessible."

They all turned as Sarah began to clap. "This is music to my ears, guys. If everyone thought like you, we'd have a lot fewer problems."

"*You* don't look tired, Sarah," Ms. Wright observed.

"I do this every day, remember?"

"When do we eat, Ms. Wright?" Izzy wore his hungriest, most pitiful look.

"I guess we could start. We should wait for Gary, but he had to pick someone up first."

"A girlfriend?" Julie asked slyly. "Do we get to meet her?"

They were already on their second helpings of burgers and salad when Gary arrived.

The doorbell rang. Shane went to answer it. He returned to the room with an odd expression on his face. "They're here." Behind him were Gary and his guest.

Jake jumped to his feet. "Kathy! What are you doing here?" He stared in puzzlement at his sister.

"Gary's date is your *sister*?" Andrew leaned back in his chair with a sly expression. "Well, well, well, isn't that interesting?"

"Hi, Jake." Kathy walked across the room to ruffle her little brother's hair. "Surprised to see me?"

"You could say that."

"Gary stopped by the free clinic where I work after the *Live!* crew did the feature on it. We had you in common, s. . . ." Kathy smiled slyly.

She looked very much like Jake at that moment with sandy blond hair and smokey eyelashes that seemed to go on forever. It was no wonder Gary had invited her out.

"You're one lucky guy, Jake," Andrew interjected smoothly. "It must be nice to have your sister dating someone with influence. I suppose you'll get all the cushy jobs on *Live!* from now on."

Jake's ears turned bright pink.

"Yeah! He'll probably be sleeping in one of the editing bays while we do all the work."

"You aren't going to play favorites, are you, Gary?"

The teasing was relentless. Both Jake and Gary looked embarrassed and helpless. Only Kathy didn't seem to mind.

"Are you picking on my baby brother?" she asked. "Because, if you are, I might have to set you guys straight." She curled her fists and set them on her hips. She looked about as dangerous as a kitten.

"Aw, he can take it. Can't you, Jake?"

The teasing dissolved into laughter as Izzy's baby doll burst into heart-wrenching wails.

"I can't even eat a meal without that thing going off!" Izzy pulled at the doll's blankets.

"Now you know what it's like to be a parent," Rosie observed.

"It's a pain in the neck." Izzy thrust the key into the doll's back to stop its cries. "My time isn't my own. I have to jump every time this thing cries. It's ruining my social life. . . ." His voice trailed away. "But that's kind of the point, isn't it? Better I figure that out now rather than get tied down with a *real* kid while I'm in high school."

"Apparently the program is working," Ms. Wright said. "More potato salad? Beans?"

"Gary told me a little about your project," Kathy said. "Tell me about your day. What did you learn?"

"I thought I'd have a harder time getting around," Josh said. "The stores are more accessible than I thought they'd be. I ran into trouble a couple times, but not as much as I'd expected. I did try to go through a revolving door, but it didn't work. My chair wouldn't fit."

"I'd have to agree with Josh," Darby said. "One of my big problems was the door of the ladies rest room. It was so heavy I could hardly get it open. The only other difficulty I had was with carpeting. Jake had to push me on carpet. I wasn't strong enough to do it myself."

"It was weird at lunch time," Kate added. "The Food Court got very crowded and people were bumping into me. They were so busy looking up at the menu signs that they didn't even notice I was down there. If people *did* notice me, they stared. It would have been much nicer if someone had smiled occasionally."

Sarah nodded in agreement as the others spoke. "I'd much rather that people be curious about my disability than ignore it or pretend it doesn't exist. I don't want people to be afraid of me or my chair. I wish they'd talk to me. Just because I'm in this chair doesn't mean I'm not a person."

"When we were in one of the department stores, someone yelled, 'Wheelchair coming through!' It made me feel like a freak. I wished they'd just let me get around by myself!"

"And didn't you hate it when someone would touch your chair or try to push you aside?" Darby added. "It was almost as though they were touching my body! I discovered I liked it best if people said, 'May I help you?' before they tried."

"How about salesclerks?" Andrew wondered. "Did you have any trouble with them?"

"Most were great. I was impressed. One cool guy brought me the shoes I asked to try on, took them out of the box and handed them to me to look at just like I was any other customer. He was so professional that I asked him if he waited on a lot of people in wheelchairs. He said that when he'd come to work in that store, he'd been told that if someone came in a wheelchair to talk directly to the person, not the party pushing the chair. He said they were given all sorts of tips about being polite and told to treat everyone the same. I was impressed. I'm going back to that place next time I need shoes."

"How about you two?" Ms. Wright looked at Andrew and Shane.

"It was pretty much the same. We've decided we made store clerks nervous with our crutches and cane though. One lady thought I was going to wipe out a whole row of dishes with my crutch."

Shane nodded in agreement as Andrew spoke.

Gary turned to Sarah. "You've been awfully quiet through all of this. Any comments?"

"What I want to know," Kate blurted, "is how can you *stand* it?"

"If I were you, I think I'd go crazy being tied to that wheelchair," Julie added. "I'm surprised you ever smile at all. All I'd be able to think about is how to get away from that chair. How *do* you stay so cheerful when your life is so depressing?"

Molly gasped at Julie's blunt words but they didn't seem to faze Sarah in the least. In fact, the question appeared to amuse her. Everyone in the room grew very quiet, waiting for Sarah's answer.

"Believe it or not, my life's not so depressing," she said softly. "In fact, most of the time my life is really pretty great. I've got good parents, new friends like the *Live!* staff, a van. . . ."

"That doesn't answer my question," Julie responded. "I saw how it was for Kate today. We had a terrible time trying on clothes or getting her wheelchair close to the perfume counter. People tried to stare at her while pretending they didn't know she was there. I could tell others were wondering what had happened to put her in a wheelchair. It was creepy."

"You get used to that part," Sarah assured her. "It *is* creepy for a while—especially when you're wondering yourself how you managed to get into a mess like this. But with time those feelings fade and you learn a few things about yourself and about others."

"Like what?"

"Like the fact that you either have to accept that you are in a wheelchair or you'll go crazy. That people respond better to a smile than to a frown. That maybe you have an especially important job to do *because* you're in that chair."

"Huh?"

Sarah looked intensely thoughtful, as though she were trying hard to formulate the thoughts in her head. "You all know I'm a Christian," she said finally.

"What does that have to do with anything?" Kate had never been much impressed with Christians and was fairly vocal about her opinion.

"Me—in a wheelchair—smiling, happy, being the

best that I can be—might be the only sermon some people ever hear—or see."

The room was silent.

Izzy was the first to speak. His voice was low and rough with emotion. "You mean that you think you can be a better Christian witness from that wheelchair than you could be walking around on normal legs?"

"If people see me functioning and happy and, like Kate and Julie, wonder how I have managed to do it, there's a chance that they'll realize that I get my strength and ability from a Source higher than myself. If I weren't a Christian, I know the last couple years would have made me bitter and angry. I get that way sometimes anyway. I can't help it. I'm human."

" 'The only sermon someone might ever see . . .' " Izzy rolled the words across his tongue. "I like it."

Julie and Kate looked embarrassed. "I guess we never thought of your handicap in quite that way," Julie admitted. "Makes me feel a little second rate."

Sarah shook her head. "Don't feel that way. It's taken me a long time to get to this point. Sometimes still I get down." She looked to Molly and Darby. They were all remembering the night Sarah's spirits were so low. "But I only admit it to my good friends."

Izzy looked at Sarah with an admiring gaze. "You're awesome, Sarah."

Molly nudged Darby with her elbow and gave a big wink at the glow on Sarah's face. The energy sparking between Izzy and Sarah electrified the room.

"Who needs a new hairdo?" Darby whispered.

"Sarah's already got what it takes."

"And, from the looks of things," Molly whispered back, "she's also going to have Izzy—in the palm of her hand!"

CHAPTER **11**

LIVE

FROM BRENTWOOD HIGH

"Do you think we'll need more salsa?" Molly peered into a sombrero-shaped bowl at a mound of chopped tomatoes and peppers.

Darby picked up a chip and put it in her mouth. "Not unless someone brings a semi-truckload of tortilla chips. You've got enough food here to feed the entire city of Brentwood!"

"How about pizzas? We could order a couple more to have on hand just in case. . . ."

"Molly, everything is fine. The house looks great. The food is spectacular. The music is perfect. What more could you want for a party?"

"People. What if no one comes? Then what will we do? I can't eat all this salsa!" The panic in Molly's voice grew. "I should never have planned for so much food! It will all go to waste. . . ."

"You haven't given a lot of parties, have you, Molly?"

"Can you tell? Maybe I'm not cut out to be a hostess. You should have had this party. You're so calm. . . ."

Darby burst out laughing. Molly was so surprised

that she clamped her mouth shut and stared at her friend.

"Are you listening to how you sound?" Darby asked.

"Like an idiot?" Molly ventured.

"Close. Just cool off and relax. Everyone will be here. No one wants to miss a party."

"But this is important. We want Sarah to really get to know some guys. I know Izzy's a promising prospect, but if that falls through. . . ."

"She will. Don't worry." Darby took another chip. "Actually, I think that Kate and Julie are beginning to appreciate her. Neither one of them is very receptive to Sarah's talk about her faith, but I think they're really beginning to see who Sarah is as a person. If she can get through to those two, she can make friends with anyone."

"Kate and Julie are different. She sees them every day. If you're around Sarah on a regular basis, you can't help but like her. These are *guys* we're talking about. You know how they are—always looking for the prettiest, most popular girl. . . ."

"They aren't all that shallow, Molly. Look on the bright side."

Before Darby could say more the doorbell rang.

Molly gave a nervous squeal. "Oh, somebody's actually here!"

"Aren't you curious who it is? Or are you going to let them sit on the front porch?"

Molly rushed to the door and squeaked with pleasure. Six people were on the front step and several more were coming up the sidewalk.

"You're late," Molly accused when Sarah finally arrived.

"I know. I'm sorry. I had to drive Mom to the mall at the last minute. I hope you started without me."

"This party is for you, you know. There are lots of great guys here I want you to meet."

"I'm a little uncomfortable with this," Sarah said. "I wish you weren't trying to fix me up with someone. Relationships can't be rushed, you know."

Molly waved a hand in the air and disregarded Sarah's comment. "Come and meet everyone. The entire crew of *Live!* is here. . . ."

"I wonder where Izzy went? He's never late for a party where they're serving free food," Darby said much later.

"Maybe he had to baby-sit for his little sisters," Molly referred to the twins Heidi and Rachel. "You know how those two can wrap him around their little fingers. He's probably playing with them until bed-time."

"I hope so. It's not like Izzy not to show up for something he agreed to attend." Darby glanced at the clock. It was ten-fifteen.

At eleven, the doorbell rang. When Molly opened the door, Izzy bolted inside. He looked dreadful.

His hair, which was never very traditional looking, looked as though it had been electrocuted strand by strand. His clothes were wrinkled and his socks didn't match. The tail of his shirt was stuffed into only half of his waistband. His eyes were bleary and clouded and dark circles like huge thumbprints hung beneath his eyes.

Under one arm, Isador carried his baby.

"What's wrong with you?" Andrew wondered as he sauntered by the foyer. "Car wreck? Hurricane? Lightning strike?"

"Worse!" Izzy thrust the doll out in front of him as though it were crawling with spiders. "This brat cried all night! It woke me up at three this morning and it's been fussing and yelling off and on ever since. I called the Home Living teacher and she said my baby was probably simulating a child with an earache and that the only thing I could do was to keep the key turned in its back! I'm exhausted. I have a headache. My grandmother and mother won't have anything to do with this doll. Even my little sisters won't take care of it! They say it's too 'noisy.' What am I supposed to do? I can't leave it unattended but it's driving me crazy. . . ."

Izzy sagged wearily against the door jamb. "I'm never going to have kids. Never. Ever."

"Don't say that. You can't tell from just one experience with a fussy toy from a Home Living class."

"I can understand how parents could lose it with a crying baby," Izzy said. "There should be classes and support groups for parents of young children. They should come with instruction manuals. People should be told in advance what to expect before having a baby!"

"Isn't that what's happening to you?" Darby wondered.

"I'll never think about kids in the same way again. I've never felt so helpless, out of control or tied down in my entire life. Everything revolves around this doll. It determines when I eat, when I sleep, when I do my homework. I even have to schedule my shower around it!" He looked down at the sweet-faced infant. "Oh, sure, now it's smiling—after it's ruined my life!"

"You'll be able to turn that doll in soon, won't you?" Darby asked.

"Not nearly soon enough."

"Just think about the teenagers who have *real* babies. There's nowhere for them to turn in a real baby and receive a grade!"

"Darby's right," Molly said. "Just yesterday I heard about a pregnant girl in the senior class. Sad, huh?"

Izzy straightened. He looked upset. "Really? I'm sure she doesn't know what she's gotten herself into. Kids should be more careful. They have no business having sex before marriage and bringing a new life into the world. It takes *at least* two people to care for a baby." He eyed the doll. "Maybe even three or four. Good grades usually come easy for me, but I'm stumped by this little thing. What if it were *real*?"

At that moment, the doll began to wail.

"Oh no! Not again. Not now, Junior!" Izzy stuffed the doll under his arm so that he could use both hands to search through his pocket for the key. Frantically he patted his pockets.

"What's going on out here?" Grady O'Brien, a friend from nearby Braddington, asked. Four other guys stood behind him. All were staring at the doll.

Izzy was drawing a crowd.

"Is that one of those dolls from the Home Living class? I've heard about them. Can I take a look?"

"Hold it while I find the key to shut it off." Izzy thrust the doll away from himself.

"Take that thing outside," Kate yelled. "It's making too much noise. We can't hear ourselves think!"

"Who says she's able to 'think' anyway?" someone muttered but the group of boys moved toward the door.

"Maybe we could muffle the sound with some masking tape over its mouth. . . ."

"Leave my doll alone!" Izzy yelped. "I've got the key right here . . . somewhere . . . if you give me a minute I'll find it. . . ."

The group of boys left the house still entranced by the mechanical noise machine. They settled on the front lawn, laughing and passing the doll from one pair of arms to another.

Inside, Molly stamped her fists and gave an angry squeal. "Oh, that makes me so mad!"

"Now what?"

"Izzy's baby is ruining all the fun!"

"But that's the point, isn't it?" said Darby with a comical smile. "Real babies aren't very welcome at parties for teens either."

"Fine. But don't you see? It's ruining everything. All the guys are outside with Izzy fooling with that doll. All the girls are inside talking."

"That happens at parties sometimes."

"But I didn't want it to happen at this one! I had a point to get across at this party. Sarah looks absolutely fantastic tonight. Her hair and make-up are perfect. Her outfit is darling."

"Your point?"

"Nobody—no *boy*—is noticing because of Isador's doll! I wanted her to meet some guys and to build a little self-confidence where boys are concerned. How can that happen when all they want to look at is Izzy's baby?"

"Who's got the key to editing room B? Andrew, can you run the toaster for today's show? Jake, set up more chairs in the studio. . . ."

"Must have had extra sugar on your cereal this morning, Molly," Jake commented lazily. "You're a little hyper, aren't you?"

"She's *hyper*-hyper!" Kate grumbled. "She's got me on the character generator and she's changed things a dozen times already."

Molly scraped her frizzy blond hair out of her eyes. "Sorry, but there are a lot of people coming to the studio today, and I want everything to run smoothly. I'm in charge today and it will reflect badly on me if you guys mess up."

"She sure told us," Jake said, suppressing a grin. Kate snorted and stomped away, her black hair swinging behind her like an inky wave.

"I'm sorry I'm so uptight. It's just that I want this to be so perfect. I feel like this story is too important for us to be casual about it."

"Who's coming in today?" Darby wondered. She'd been putting up with Molly's nerves all morning and was feeling a little frayed around the edges herself.

"First it will be three handicapped students from here at Brentwood High. Sarah will be in that group. They will be interviewed by Josh. He's going to ask them how it is to be a handicapped or physically-challenged person here at the high school. Next, three 'normal' students will be interviewed. They'll be asked to express their attitudes, opinions, and responses toward handicapped students. After that, Josh will moderate a forum for all six students and have them discuss their feelings and opinions together."

"It sounds great. Josh will do a beautiful job. You have nothing to worry about."

"Oh, yes I do." Molly tugged on her hair again. "Shane was in charge of getting the interviewees. He had to find five students willing to talk to us in this format."

"You sound apprehensive."

"I am. Who knows what circle Shane runs with these days? You know his reputation isn't the best."

"But he always has perfect manners in here."

"That doesn't mean his friends and acquaintances will."

"*We're* his 'friends and acquaintances' too."

"Oh, Darby, you know what I mean. Until he started working with *Live!* Shane was always on the fringes of trouble. You know that."

Darby did. She'd had a crush on Shane for several months during the last school year. Fortunately Shane had never really known how she'd felt and now—partially because of Jake—that interest had simmered to mere friendship. Shane's reputation included his being very careless with the girls in his life.

"Just because people who don't know him think of him as a wild boy doesn't mean that he won't get good people to interview."

"Ms. Wright insisted that he should do it all by himself," Molly continued unplacated.

"Maybe she wants to build his confidence."

"And ruin my nerves!"

"Who's going to co-anchor with Josh?"

"Jake. That's the only thing that's kept me from going crazy. He'll probably be able to handle anybody Shane brings in."

"You're borrowing trouble. Shane's great. Trust him. I think you're worrying for nothing. Shane isn't the kind who'd set out to make problems for others. He's been nothing but considerate here in the media room."

Molly didn't agree. Her brow furrowed. "I'm not so sure. He scares me sometimes. He's so sullen. It's as though you never know what's going on in his mind. He hardly ever smiles. And have you *ever* seen him laugh?" She turned to Sarah who was sitting quietly nearby. "Well, *have* you?"

"Maybe once or twice, but not often," Sarah admitted. "But do you think anyone has given Shane enough of a chance? You sound like you're judging him, Molly, and you have no idea how he'll do."

"Maybe so, Sarah. I'm not as nice as you are to people, but I have this bad feeling...."

Their conversation was interrupted when Gary walked into the room and it erupted into a cacophony of whistles and catcalls. "Gary and Kathy, sitting in a tree, K-I-S-S-I-N-G. First comes love, then comes marriage, then comes Gary with a *baby carriage*," Josh chanted.

"Maybe they can have Izzy's baby. That would convince them never to have any children," Julie added.

"Having *Izzy* around should convince someone never to have any children!" Andrew looked smug.

"Ignore them," Molly advised Sarah who was sitting very quietly. "The testosterone levels in this room are much too high. Everybody is edgy. They're letting off steam by teasing. I'll be glad when this show is over."

"It's not the guys," Sarah murmured. "I'm—believe it or not—used to them."

"What is it then?" Darby pulled a stool nearer to Sarah's chair.

"Nothing."

"You aren't a good liar, Sarah, so don't even try."

"Nothing that makes sense, then."

"Try us. Maybe we can help you make sense of what you're thinking."

"I've been in this very strange mood ever since we started working on this story. You know that."

"That's understandable. It hits close to home where you're concerned. How people view the handicapped is very important to your life."

"It's something else. That part, at least, makes sense. Lately I've had more trouble handling the *emotional* side of my situation than the physical one."

"I don't get it," Molly said honestly. "What could

be harder than to find yourself paralyzed and in a wheelchair?"

"*Accepting* that you're paralyzed and in a wheelchair, that's what. I went through all the anger and denial the psychologists predicted. I finally came to acknowledge that the chair wasn't going to go away and that my legs weren't going to start working. I thought I had it all behind me and then. . . ."

Darby took Sarah's hand in her own and gave it a squeeze of encouragement.

"And then just lately I realized that being a 'normal' teenager was totally impossible for me and I've felt as though I lost my legs—and myself—all over again."

"Why do you feel that way? That you can't be a 'normal' teenager, I mean?"

"You know perfectly well. You tried to help me. We re-did my hair, my look. Molly had a party so I could meet new people. Nothing helped. I'm still just 'that girl in the wheelchair.' Sometimes I'm that 'Christian in the wheelchair,' but other than that, nothing changes."

Sarah's gentle green eyes clouded. "Why can't people appreciate who I am? Why do they always have to be put off by the wheelchair and my disability? What else can I do?"

She was on the verge of tears when Gary sauntered over to ask her a question about the story package she and Andrew had done a week earlier. Molly and Darby moved away.

"What are we going to do?" Molly agonized. "She is probably the sweetest, kindest person I've ever known in my entire life. Why can't guys see that? Why can't *everyone* see it?"

"I don't know," Darby said helplessly. "We've tried. I can understand a little of what Sarah must feel—frustrated, lonely, powerless. It's as though that wheelchair forms a little glass house around her that very few people try to enter even though she's on the inside welcoming them. If people were more mature they'd look past the chair to see the beautiful person inside."

"I'd be frustrated too if guys thought I was invisible. What's high school for if you can't interact with the opposite sex?"

"Studying?" Darby offered with mild humor.

"Oh, that. Sure, but the fun—" Molly was distracted by a commotion at the door.

Izzy arrived in his usual flurry. Today, however, there was something dramatically different about his entrance. Izzy was pushing a stroller. Over one arm was a fuzzy blue blanket. Over the other were the handles of what looked suspiciously like a diaper bag.

Andrew opened his mouth to speak but Izzy gave him such a withering glare that Andrew's mouth snapped shut again.

"Don't even say it," Izzy growled. "Not one word. Not even a syllable."

Gary, however, was not intimidated. "What's in the bag, Big Guy? Is it what I think it is? Diapers?"

Izzy's head drooped. "No. Toys. And water in a bottle."

"I can understand bringing the doll with you, but the rest. . . ."

"My little sisters insisted. They're really into this doll thing. They had the toy bag ready when I left for school. I thought I could dump this whole mess in my locker and forget it but nothing will fit. I didn't realize how narrow my locker is. Besides, I built some shelves in there to hold my books and I can't get them out. I must have nailed something to the back wall. Anyway, I couldn't get this junk into the locker so I thought maybe I could keep it down here at Chaos Central until it's time to go home."

"Why not?" Gary said with a chuckle. "We're all beginning to get attached to Junior. Think of us as one big, happy family."

"Thanks." Izzy looked supremely relieved. He gave the stroller a kick and it went flying into the corner. "Now all I have to do is to figure out what to do about tomorrow night."

"What's happening then?" Molly asked.

"I promised my grandmother I'd take her to a birthday party at the Senior Center. It's being given for one of her best friends. Mom and Dad are taking the girls shopping for new shoes. There won't be anyone at home to take care of the doll. Gram has already said I can't take it with me. She says that everywhere I go with that doll there's trouble. She doesn't want us ruining the party for her friend." Izzy looked morose. "I can hardly blame her. Still, I've stuck it out this far. I don't want to leave the doll now."

"Hire a baby-sitter."

"I tried. People either think I'm nuts or they're busy. I didn't know how difficult it was to find a sitter on a school night. Everybody's at sports practice or music lessons or gymnastics. Don't kids ever stay home anymore? How do they plan to earn their spending money if they won't take baby-sitting jobs?"

"You sound just like my mom," Josh said. "We tell her she sounds like an old lady when she talks like that."

Izzy looked more depressed than ever. "This doll is ruining my life! What am I going to do?"

"I'll baby-sit for you, Izzy." Sarah's soft voice was barely audible over the noise in the room.

"Huh?" Izzy spun around on his heels to stare at her. "What'd you say?"

"I'll take the doll. I'm not doing anything tomorrow night. I'd be happy to help you out."

It was touch and go for a moment whether or not Izzy was going to give Sarah a big, grateful kiss on the lips. "You will? You mean it?"

"Of course. Just bring it over and show me what to do."

"It's been crying a lot. Very fussy. A colicky baby."

"That's fine. I've been warned."

Izzy laid the doll in Sarah's arms. Then he took the handgrips of her wheelchair and pushed her toward a quieter corner of the room where they became engrossed in an animated conversation.

"Can you believe this?" Molly said. "We have a show to do and Shane's unknown guests to interview—and they're having a heart-to-heart about a doll! Is everyone *planning* to ruin my life or is it just working out that way?"

"I told you that you didn't have to worry," Darby said after the final interview was complete. "Shane's guests were great. Some of the best we've had. Insightful. Smart. It was a terrific program."

"It was, wasn't it?" Molly wore a self-satisfied grin.

"Don't take all the credit," Jake whispered as he walked by. "I overheard you spazzing about Shane's guests."

Molly made a face. "I underestimated him, that's all."

"I think we all have."

CHAPTER 13

LIVE
FROM DRENTWOOD HIGH

"Where do you suppose she is?" Molly muttered, peeking through the drapes in Darby's living room for the fifteenth time. "Sarah's never late. You could set your watch by her! Do you think she had trouble with her van?"

"She said she wanted to study with us tonight but she didn't say *exactly* what time she'd be coming. Actually, she was a little evasive. I think she had something going on before she came here." Darby paused to consider. "When I talked to her she sounded ... funny."

"What's that supposed to mean?" Molly reshuffled her books and papers absentmindedly.

"I don't know. Just funny. Usually Sarah is up front but today she didn't tell me what she was doing. It couldn't have been bad, though, because she sounded happy. Almost giddy."

"Weird. I suppose she'll tell us when she gets here. *If* she ever gets here!

"By the way," Molly continued, her mind already racing on to other things, "what do you think of Gary going out with Jake's sister Kathy?"

"It's fine with me. They're both great people. Actually, I'm glad. Gary's such a loner. Kathy will be good for him."

"But how does Jake feel about it?"

"He says his sister is a big girl and can take care of herself. He's used to his sisters dating, although this is the first time that any of them have dated someone this close to him."

"I think it's romantic," Molly concluded. "Too bad my life isn't romantic."

Darby was saved by the doorbell from a recitation of Molly's dating woes—most of which involved Andrew Tremaine.

"There's Sarah!" Molly jumped to her feet and hurried to the door.

Darby blinked as Sarah rolled into the room. "Sarah! What's happened to you?"

"Nothing. Why?"

"You . . . how you look . . . you're glowing!"

The bright tinkle of Sarah's laughter filled the room. "Like a light bulb?"

"Almost. You look positively radiant. Where have you been?"

"In the park, playing Frisbee."

"*I* never look like that when I'm done playing Frisbee."

"Who were you with?" Molly took up the interrogation. "And how do you play Frisbee from a wheelchair, anyway?"

"I was with Izzy. And you play it just like you play

it on your feet—only slower and you miss more often."

"Izzy? *Our* Izzy? Isador Eugene Mooney?"

"That's the one."

"Tell me more." Darby put her hands on her hips and grinned at Sarah.

"He asked me out, that's all."

"On a *date*?"

"You could call it that."

"A *real* date?"

"Real as they come."

"You went on your very first date ever with Izzy?" Molly gave an ear-piercing shriek and Darby joined her. They both hugged Sarah and laughed.

"Tell us how this happened," Darby ordered. "Every detail."

Sarah's hands fluttered to her cheeks. "Remember when I offered to baby-sit for Izzy's doll? That night, when he came to pick it up, he asked me what kinds of things I liked to do. I told him I enjoyed plays and concerts, sports, playing games, goofing off in the park, that kind of thing.

"He seemed surprised at first but then said it sounded as though I liked to do some of the same things he enjoyed. That's when he asked me if I wanted to have a picnic supper with him in the park tonight."

"Oh, cool! Izzy's smoother than I thought!" Molly appeared delighted.

"It was very sweet. He brought a basket with fried chicken, salad, and lemonade. He said his grandmother made it for him. We ate and talked and then he pulled out a Frisbee. We tossed it back and forth. If I missed it, he went loping after it like a big puppy." Sarah clapped her hands. "I loved it!"

She grew a little pensive. "I felt so *normal*."

"Who'd have thought?" Darby murmured. *"Izzy."*

"Before we did the latest story Izzy didn't even think of dating me," Sarah said. "He admitted it. He told me that it had never entered his mind—mostly because I was in a wheelchair and he didn't know what someone did with a person in a chair. It wasn't until we began to work on this story that he realized he was hurting himself by not getting to know me better. We talked about the prejudices he had and how this story opened his eyes."

Her eyes filmed with tears. "He even apologized for overlooking me. Izzy said that he had no idea how many 'normal' things I was interested in or liked to do."

"That big old teddy bear of a guy has a heart," Molly observed. "I knew it."

"We're going to a ball game next," Sarah said. "I'm going to show him the ropes of getting around the stadium in a wheelchair."

"How does it feel?" Darby wondered. "To be dating, I mean."

"Normal," Sarah responded. "And sometimes there's nothing that feels better than being ordinary and average, everyday and typical. I can guarantee it."

———

When Izzy walked into the media room, Sarah looked up from the book she was reading. His smile grew so wide it threatened to split his face in two. Sarah's was equally enthusiastic.

"Do you think they're glad to see each other?" Molly whispered to Darby.

"Just a little. It's as though someone turned an extra light on in the room."

"I love it," Molly cooed.

"Izz-man, are you still carrying that thing around?" Shane referred to the baby doll under Izzy's arm.

"I get to turn it in today. I'd better get an A in this class after all I've suffered. Lack of sleep, nervous tension, stress. . . ."

"Just like a real father?" Ms. Wright asked.

Izzy thought about the question for a moment. "Yeah, I guess so. I never realized how hard a father's job could be."

"So you'll be glad to dump the brat, right?" Andrew said bluntly.

"Yes. And no."

"*No?* I can't believe you said that!"

"It will be a relief to get rid of the responsibility and the crying and the noise," Izzy said, "but I'll kind of miss the silly thing too. I got lots of attention from girls when I was carrying or strolling it. Ladies smiled at me. Little kids always wanted to look at the baby. In a crazy sort of way I got attached to it."

Izzy sank into a chair and cradled the doll in his arms. "For the first time, I'm aware of what it means to be a parent. That's not saying I have the full picture, but I am starting to understand the responsibility and even some of the pleasure of parenting."

"From a plastic doll?"

"I've tried to think of it as more than that. I've tried to pretend it was a real baby and ask myself how I'd feel or react if it were my honest-to-goodness child crying. That's pretty heavy-duty stuff."

He gave a little shudder. "The first thing I realized is that I'm not old enough for that kind of responsibility. I want to have some fun first. Go to school. Enjoy my freedom. *Then* get married and have children."

"I thought you said you didn't want children after this experience," Andrew reminded him.

"I didn't, not at first. Now I've changed my mind. Still, I'll think about it long and hard. Something Sarah said keeps sticking in my mind."

Sarah looked up, surprised. "What did I say?"

"You said that people should realize that when they have a child they should never be careless about it because they're bringing an entirely new life and new soul into the world—one that will be around for eternity.

"If it's true, that a person does have a soul and it is around for eternity, then we'd better never take having a child for granted—right?"

"You think too much, Izz-man," Andrew said. "That's too heavy for me. I think you and Sarah belong together."

Izzy gave Sarah a long, warm look. "You know, Andrew, for once, I think you're right."

Ms. Wright clapped her hands. "Since everyone is here, I'd like for us to have a discussion about the story we just finished. It's had very good reception from the people who viewed it. I'd like to know if working on this package has changed any attitudes or ideas for any of you." She looked around the room. "Who wants to go first? Izzy? Sarah? Has anything changed for you?"

Ms. Wright looked confused when Izzy blushed to the roots of his hair and Sarah's pale complexion darkened. Shane and Jake sniggered.

"You bet their lives changed!" Molly said under her breath. Sensing that her question hadn't been perfectly timed, Ms. Wright continued.

"Are there any ways you can be more helpful or compassionate to the physically challenged?"

"Treat them like you treat everyone else."

"Don't stare. Smile instead."

"Show them respect."

"Don't act like their disability is a disease that could be caught. Don't shy away."

Ideas spilled out from around the room.

The noon bell rang and Izzy stood up. "I've got a great idea. Take someone in a wheelchair to lunch." He looked at Sarah and she smiled and nodded. Then Izzy put his hands on the handgrips of Sarah's chair and wheeled her toward the door.

Shane murmured, "Way to go, Izzy." Jake began to clap. Kate and Julie cheered.

Ms. Wright didn't even attempt to hide her smile.

"Well," she finally said as she closed up her grade book, "that's what's so interesting about working in television. You just never know where a story will take you!"

———————

Live's latest story is about a part of the youth prison system—"last chance" ranches for troubled boys. Shane's interest becomes very personal when he discovers one of his former friends is an inmate. While researching the kinds of vandalism some of these boys have committed, Izzy becomes intrigued with graffiti and discovers that sometimes there is a true artist lurking in the dark corners of a troubled youth.

Turn the page for an exciting
Sneak Preview
of

Silent Thief

Book #23 in the
CEDAR RIVER DAYDREAMS series
by Judy Baer

CEDAR RIVER DAYDREAMS

Silent
Thief

Judy Baer

Chapter One

Binky McNaughton stared intently into the mirror in Lexi Leighton's bedroom. She frowned and grimaced before her features settled into a full scowl of disgust. With quick, jerky motions she grasped wisps of her reddish brown hair, piled them on top of her head, and studied the effect in the mirror. The scraggly hairdo resembled a haystack. As quickly as she'd put it up, she allowed her hair to tumble back to her shoulders. The expression on her face soured even more.

Peggy Madison, who was watching Binky from across the room, rolled her eyes and turned to Lexi. "Where's your mom today? I didn't see her when we came in."

"Mom's locked herself in the studio. She's getting ready for her first solo art show."

"At the gallery downtown?" Peggy sounded impressed. "Don't they bring people from all over the country to show in that gallery?"

"It has a good reputation. That's why Mom is

working so hard on her paintings. This show is her big chance."

"Does this mean your mother's going to be famous?" Binky took time away from the mirror. "If she is, I'd better get her autograph now. She probably won't want to give it to me later."

"Well, she may not be famous, but it will increase the value of her artwork. That usually happens when an artist's reputation grows. Mom's excited. She never thought she'd get this far with her art."

"Just think," Peggy said, "we *know* her. I bet she *will* be famous someday. Her work will probably hang in the biggest art galleries in the world and we'll be able to say that our best friend is her daughter."

Binky didn't respond. She was too busy looking in the mirror to pay attention to the ongoing conversation. She splayed her fingers and touched the edges of her face just next to her ears. Then she lifted the skin until it was pulled tight across the bridge of her nose.

"Oh no!" A squeak of dismay erupted from her. She leaned forward until her nose nearly touched the mirror. "A zit on the end of my nose!" She looked cross-eyed toward its tip. "Can you believe it? Do you think I should squeeze it? Don't answer that. I don't want to know. I don't want to think about it." Binky glared at her reflection and stuck out her tongue.

"I have to ask," Lexi finally weakened. "I've

been watching you do goofy things to your face for the last fifteen minutes. What in the world are you doing?"

"Other than losing her mind?" Jennifer Golden was sprawled across Lexi's bed paging through magazines.

"It's time to send Binky away for a rest. She's losing it. There's no doubt about it."

Binky ignored them to examine a minuscule roll of fat she'd found at the waistband of her jeans. "Look at this blubber." She pinched a tiny flap of skin between her fingers and shook it.

"Look at what? I don't see anything," Lexi challenged.

"I'm a mess. I have a zit on my nose, fat at my waist, unhealthy skin. My color's bad too—don't you think it's grayish? I should drink more water. That might help. Drinking water flushes the impurities from your body. One problem with drinking all that water is that I'll have to go to the bathroom all the time. And Egg always hogs the bathroom at our house. I don't know what he does in there. Homework, I think. . . ."

"Binky, you're being even weirder than usual and that's *pretty weird*," Peggy observed.

"Just look at me." Binky turned away from the mirror and spread her hands wide.

"You're the same as always," Jennifer said.

Binky's eyes filled with tears. "I know. Isn't it awful?" She sank onto the edge of Lexi's bed, her shoulders drooping. She looked disconsolate. "I look terrible. I didn't realize what bad shape I was in until I visited Harry at college."

"So that's what this is all about," Peggy crowed. "Harry."

"No, it's not about Harry. It's about me. While I was on campus, everywhere I went I saw beautiful girls. Blondes, brunettes, redheads. Tall ones, short ones. All of them gorgeous. They looked so sophisticated and put together and . . . healthy. When I look in the mirror, I don't like what I see."

"Binky, you're perfectly good-looking and you know it." Lexi tried to sound reassuring.

"There's more to this than just seeing a bunch of beautiful girls on Harry's college campus," Jennifer muttered. "What's the *real* problem here?"

"I can't compete," Binky said in a tiny voice. "There's *no way* I can compete for Harry's attention with all those beautiful girls around. I'm surprised he calls or writes to me at all. Why should he? Every one of the girls I met was spectacular. They all looked as though they'd been working out at a gym or in-line skating six hours a day. I look so . . ." Binky searched for a word that would describe her. "Blah!"

"Binky, you look fine," Peggy said.

"No, I don't. You're saying that because you're my friend and you think you *have* to say it.

"I need a new look," Binky continued. "Something that will keep Harry interested in me. We hardly ever get to see each other and he's with those beautiful girls every single day. There has to be something about me that's special, that will keep me in his mind even when we're apart."

Jennifer snorted loudly. "Harry *has* to be interested in you, Binky. No one ever knows what you're going to do next. You're the perfect mystery woman."

"She's right," Peggy added. "Personality plus, Binky. That's you. Why would Harry *want* any other girl when he can have you?"

Binky refused to be convinced. She picked up a magazine. "Magazines always have self-improvement programs in them, don't they?" she mused. "*That*'s what I need! I'm going to start a self-improvement program. 'Firm and Tone Your Thighs in Twenty Minutes a Day.' " Binky propped the magazine open on the floor next to her. "And here's an article telling me how to have glowing skin in only fifteen minutes a day. I can do that. 'Walk Your Way to Good Health in an Hour a Day.' That's a good one."

"Wait a minute," Jennifer said. "If you spend twenty minutes on your thighs, an hour walking, fifteen minutes on your face, and all the other things you're probably planning, there won't be any hours in the day to go to school or see your friends. Be realistic!"

"But I have to do *something*. It's the only way I can hang on to Harry."

"It's the only way you *think* you can hang on to Harry," Lexi pointed out. "Has Harry said anything negative about your looks?"

"Of course not. He's too nice to do anything like that."

"Maybe he hasn't said anything because he knows you're fine just the way you are."

Binky wouldn't buy it. "I need a new look and I'm going to get one. I've been thinking about this for a long time. Now it's time to start."

Although Binky was prone to fits of enthusiasm, she usually lost interest in projects quickly. This time, however, she sounded serious. She and Harry Cramer had dated for a long time. If she thought there was something jeopardizing their relationship, Binky would do everything in her power to change it.

"What, exactly, are you planning?"

"Do you *really* want to hear about my self-improvement program, or are you just going to laugh at me?" Binky asked suspiciously.

"We won't laugh. We promise." As she spoke, Lexi gave Jennifer a warning stare. Jennifer had a tendency to blurt out what was on her mind, whether it was complimentary or not.

"All right, here goes." Binky pulled a tattered piece of paper out of the pocket of her jeans. "I've got a list."

Jennifer's eyebrows shot upward until they were hidden beneath her blond bangs. "A list?"

"Yes, my self-improvement list. I don't know why using this for a self-improvement program didn't occur to me before." Binky studied the page intently. "I've been compiling it ever since I got back from my visit with Harry.

"First of all, I'm not going to skip any more meals, especially not breakfast. I read that it makes your body switch into starvation mode. It's much better to eat three meals a day."

"Binky, you *never* skip a meal," Peggy pointed out. "You eat meals even when there aren't any meals to be eaten!"

"I'm also going to quit snacking. Junk food isn't good for your body. No more fat, no more salt. . . ."

"No more taste, no more flavor," Jennifer added.

"I'll just have to learn to like it," Binky said importantly.

"I read about an effective diet with only one rule to follow," Peggy offered. "If it tastes good, spit it out. If it tastes bad, swallow."

Binky gave her friend a disgusted look. "Do you want to hear the rest of my list or not?"

"I wouldn't miss it for the world."

"I'm not going to smoke."

"That shouldn't be too hard, Binky. You don't do that anyway."

"I know. And I'm never going to. It makes your skin gross, your lungs polluted, your breath bad, and your clothes stink. Besides that, if you smoke for a long time you get these little tiny cracky lines around your mouth that make you look about a thousand years old."

"Good. What else?"

"I'm going to floss my teeth every day."

"The dentists of America salute you."

"I may not be as beautiful as some of those girls on Harry's campus, but I'm going to have the best teeth. And I'm not going to drink soda anymore either . . . just water. Do you know that carbonation is hard on the calcium in your bones?"

"Thanks so much for sharing," Jennifer said. "I think I'm getting sick to my stomach."

"And I'm going to start walking every day . . . miles and miles."

"Isn't that overly ambitious?" Lexi asked doubtfully.

"Maybe I'll start with one mile. Egg can drive me to the mall and I'll walk in there."

"If you're going to have Egg drive you to the mall so you can walk, wouldn't it be simpler just to *walk* to the mall yourself?"

"I never thought of that."

"What would you do without me?" Jennifer stared helplessly at her friend.

"I'm also going to have a facial as soon as I save up enough money," Binky continued. "And I'm going to learn how to wear clothes so I don't always look like I shop at a thrift store."

"But you *do* shop at thrift stores, Binky."

She ignored the comment. "I'm going to save my money. That way, the next time I see Harry I can have a whole new wardrobe and really impress him. And I'm going to start reading books, newspapers—everything I can get my hands on—

so I sound really smart when we have conversations."

"That list should keep you busy," Lexi said.

"True. And I'll add more resolutions as I go along," Binky said. "This is just a start. I'll tell you about them when I decide what's next."

"I'm sure we're going to be hearing all about it." Binky might be the one wanting self-improvement, but none of the girls had any doubt that they'd all get sucked into her enthusiasm.

"I think your plan sounds great, Binky. I hope it works out very well." Lexi gave a cat-like stretch. "As for me, I'm starved. Mom said she was going to bake chocolate chip cookies this morning. Anybody want one?"

"Your mom makes the world's best cookies," Jennifer said. "I'll never say no."

"They're better than the ones at that cookie store in the mall," Peggy added. "Do you think she made them with macadamia nuts this time?"

A little whimper came from Binky's corner of the room. "Chocolate chip macadamia nut cookies?" She looked as though she were about to drool all over her shoes. "I *love* chocolate chip macadamia nut cookies."

"Then come downstairs and have one," Lexi invited.

"Weren't you listening to me at all?" Binky wailed. "What about my self-improvement program?"

"Binky, you're the size of a toothpick. One cookie won't hurt you."

"But I can't eat just one. You know that."

"Even four cookies won't hurt you. Come on."

"What about all the fat and the sugar?"

"Have a glass of juice while we eat," Lexi offered.

"Juice? No thanks. I'll start my self-improvement program tomorrow." A grin lit Binky's features. "That's what I'll do. I'll just start tomorrow. Come on. What are we waiting for? Let's go down and get those cookies!"

Cookies and milk in hand, the girls walked into Mrs. Leighton's cheerful studio. The room was an eclectic clutter of easels, tables, and canvases. Several paintings in various stages of completion hung on the walls. A portrait of Lexi and Ben was the focal point of the room. Mrs. Leighton, in jeans and a paint-spattered sweatshirt, was at her easel putting finishing touches on a delicate flower. Oddly, she was wearing sunglasses.

"Hello, girls. I see you found the cookies. I heard you come in after school, but I was so involved in this project I just didn't want to quit. How's it looking?"

"Great!" Jennifer said admiringly. "You're the best artist I know."

Binky concurred.

"That's very flattering. I need all the praise I can get right now. I'm a little nervous about my upcoming show."

"I hate to sound snoopy or anything, Mrs. Leighton," Binky ventured, "but why are you wearing sunglasses?"

"Oh, sorry," Mrs. Leighton slipped them off and tucked one bow into the waistband of her jeans. "How silly of me. It seemed awfully bright in here. It was easier for me to see with the glasses on, that's all."

"Mom, it's not unusually bright in here today. You're the one who likes this room because it's a northern exposure."

"It's very strange, isn't it?" Mrs. Leighton shrugged off the odd event nonchalantly. "My eyes have been bothering me lately. Perhaps I need glasses. Your father says I've been squinting a lot."

"I didn't realize you'd been having trouble with your eyes," Binky said.

"Not 'trouble,' really. It's just that when I start to paint on a white canvas, I'm bothered by the glare. It gives me a headache. I've always enjoyed the windows in this room, but lately I've wished that I'd put shades on them so I could darken it a bit."

"My mom always gets headaches when she needs her glasses changed," Peggy said.

"I'm sure that's all it is," Mrs. Leighton said lightly as her fingers drifted to her temple. "But I do have a terrible headache. Maybe I should take a break and have one of those cookies myself."

"Is that why you've been pulling the drapes in the living room lately?" Lexi wondered, refusing to be diverted. "The house is always dark when I come home from school."

"Sunshine and light fade carpets and uphol-steries, you know," Mrs. Leighton said. "I really should have been protecting the furniture all along."

"You've never cared about that before," Lexi persisted.

"You've probably been working too hard, Mrs. Leighton." Peggy glanced around the room. "This place is *filled* with artwork."

"You're right. I've been driving myself crazy trying to get enough good work done for the show."

"Is it that important?"

"It's been one of my goals to be known as a talented local artist," Mrs. Leighton admitted. "This is my first big break. If I show well here, it will establish my reputation in the community. It certainly wouldn't hurt to sell more canvases."

"I think you should get some rest," Binky interjected. "Otherwise you might get sick and not be able to do your show anyway. That's what my mom would say."

"Your mother's a very wise woman." Mrs. Leighton smiled. "And I *do* plan to rest as soon as I get this canvas completed. And after that, I'm going to have my eyes checked." She picked up her brush again and stared at the canvas. "I think a touch of umber right here would be a good idea, don't you?" Her voice trailed away as she lost herself in her work. The girls left the studio quietly.

When they reached the kitchen, Jennifer turned to Lexi. "Do you think it's weird that your mom's wearing sunglasses to paint?"

"Mom's been under a lot of strain lately," Lexi admitted. "She hasn't been herself. Dad's commented on it too. We both think she'll be better once the show is over. Then mom can get back to normal."

"What do you mean, 'normal'?" Jennifer wondered.

"Oh, nothing big. Just a lot of little things. Sometimes she complains about seeing spots before her eyes. She gets upset easily too. Once, when she'd been working all day and most of the night, she had this weird spell and couldn't see at all."

"That's scary." Binky looked alarmed.

"I know. I thought so too, but mom brushed it off like it was nothing. She's not letting anything get in the way of this art show."

"Have other weird things been happening?" Peggy appeared concerned.

"Not really. Sometimes when I come into the studio, Mom's shaking her hands—like this." Lexi demonstrated, flapping her hands limply in front of her. "She says they feel weak. I suppose that's from holding her arm at such an uncomfortable angle to paint. Sometimes her hands tremble."

"Does she have trouble walking too?" Jennifer wondered.

"Sometimes when she's really tired, I've noticed that she drags one leg. I mentioned it to her and she laughed it off. She said she was too lazy to lift it."

"She definitely needs more rest," Peggy concluded. "She's going to make herself sick if she
keeps working this hard."

"I agree with you," Lexi said somberly, "but I
don't know what to do. Mom's stubborn and in-
dependent. If she wants to work, it's pretty hard
to stop her."

"I wonder if your mother would like to join my
self-improvement program?" Binky said. "Maybe
she and I could work together on projects. It
sounds as though she needs it as much as I do!"

Cedar River Daydreams

Other Books by Judy Baer